The GHOST N[...]

ATTACK of the GRA[...]

A SHOCKER on SHOCK STREET

LET'S GET INVISIBLE

The HAUNTED CAR

The ABOMINABLE SNOWMAN OF PASADENA

The BLOB THAT ATE EVERYONE

IT CAME FROM OHIO: MY LIFE AS A WRITER

Goosebumps®
MOST WANTED

PLANET of the LAWN GNOMES

SON of SLAPPY

Goosebumps®

PLANET of the LAWN GNOMES

R.L. STINE

SCHOLASTIC

Scholastic Children's Books
An imprint of Scholastic Ltd
Euston House, 24 Eversholt Street, London, NW1 1DB, UK
Registered office: Westfield Road, Southam, Warwickshire, CV47 0RA
SCHOLASTIC and associated logos are trademarks and/or
registered trademarks of Scholastic Inc.

First published in the US by Scholastic Inc., 2012
First published in the UK by Scholastic Ltd, 2017

Copyright © Scholastic Inc., 2012

ISBN 978 1407 17881 3

Goosebumps book series created by Parachute Press, Inc

SCHOLASTIC, GOOSEBUMPS, GOOSEBUMPS HORRORLAND,
and associated logos are trademarks and/or registered trademarks of
Scholastic Inc.

A CIP catalogue record for this book
is available from the British Library.

Printed by CPI Group (UK) Ltd, Croydon, CR0 4YY
Papers used by Scholastic Children's Books are made
from wood grown in sustainable forests.

1 3 5 7 9 10 8 6 4 2

www.scholastic.co.uk

WELCOME. YOU ARE MOST WANTED.

Come in. I'm R.L. Stine. Welcome to the Goosebumps office.

I hope you didn't have trouble finding it. Did you follow my directions? "Turn left at the third open grave and follow the path through the quicksand pits."

You might think a graveyard is a strange place for an office. But I need a lot of quiet to think. And the only noise here is the sound of dead people not breathing.

Well, sit down. Just move those eyeballs out of your way. Yes, I know they're still warm and wet. I keep meaning to return them to their owners. No, they're not looking at you. Turn them the other way if they make you nervous.

Don't worry about the giant scorpion. That's Louie. He's been my pet ever since he ate my dog.

It's okay. He only craves flesh when he's hungry. Hmmm ... I can't remember. Did I feed him today?

1

Hey, don't pay any attention to those screams. Sometimes the torture chamber upstairs gets a little busy. You'll get used to it.

Yes, this is where I write all the Goosebumps books. Cozy, isn't it?

Why is my laptop covered in fur? I don't know. It didn't have fur when I bought it. Maybe I downloaded some kind of virus.

Check out that poster by the window. See those cute lawn gnomes with their funny pointed hats and their overalls and vests? The adorable painted faces?

Well, guess what? They're not so cute. They may be small — but they can make BIG trouble.

Yes, that's a WANTED poster. Those gnomes are *wanted* for being some of the most ghoulish, most evil villains in Goosebumps history.

Why am I shaking like this? I'll tell you the truth — even *I* get scared when I think back to the creepiest, crawliest, grossest villains of all time. I hope you're ready to be terrified, because I'm going to reveal their stories to you.

Yes. Here come the MOST WANTED bad guys starring in the MOST WANTED Goosebumps books.

Let's start out with these grinning, glowing-eyed lawn gnomes.

A boy named Jay Gardener can tell you all about them. Jay can tell you about the horrifying nights he spent because of these frightening statues.

They can't come to life, right?

That's what Jay thought — at first.

They're too cute to be evil?

Maybe you won't think that after you read Jay's story.

Maybe when you learn what Jay discovered late at night, you will understand why the lawn gnomes are . . . MOST WANTED.

I know I'm supposed to be careful. I know I'm supposed to be good. But sometimes you have to take a chance and hope no one is watching.

Otherwise, life would be totally boring, right?

My name is Jay Gardener. I'm twelve and sometimes I can't help it — I like a little excitement. I mean, dare me to do something — and it's done.

It's just the way I am. I'm not a bad dude. Sure, I'm in trouble a lot. I've been in some pretty bad trouble. But that doesn't mean I'm a criminal or anything.

Check out these big blue eyes. Are these the eyes of a criminal? No way. And my curly red hair? And the freckles on my nose? You might almost call me *cute*, right?

Okay, okay. Let's not get sickening about it.

My sister, Kayla, calls me Jay Bird because she says I'm as cute as a bird. Kayla is totally weird. Besides, she has the same red hair and blue eyes. So why pick on *me*?

So, okay, I felt this temptation come on. You know what that is. Just a strong feeling that you have to do something you maybe shouldn't do.

I gazed up and down our street. No one around. *Good.* No one to watch me.

The summer trees' leaves shimmered in the warm sunlight. The houses and lawns gleamed so bright, I had to squint. I stepped into the shade of Mr. McClatchy's front yard.

McClatchy lives in the big old house across the street from us. He's a mean dude and everyone hates him. He's bald and red-faced and as skinny as a toothpick. He wears his pants way up high so the belt is almost up to his armpits.

He yells at everyone in his high, shrill voice. He's always chasing kids off his lawn — even new kids, like Kayla and me. He's even mean to our dog, the sweetest golden Lab who ever lived — Mr. Phineas.

So, I had an idea to have a little fun. Of course it was wrong. Of *course* it wasn't what I was supposed to be doing. But sometimes, when you see something funny to do — you just have to take a chance.

Am I right?

That morning, I saw some guys in green uniforms doing work on the tall trees in McClatchy's front yard. When they went home, they left a ladder leaning against a tree.

I glanced up and down the street again. Still no one in sight.

I crept up to the ladder and grabbed its sides. I slid it away from the tree trunk. The ladder was tall but light. Not hard to move.

Gripping it tightly by the sides, I dragged it to the front of McClatchy's house. I leaned it against the wall. Then I slid it to the open window on the second floor.

Breathing hard, I wiped my sweaty hands on the legs of my jeans. "Sweet," I murmured. "When McClatchy comes home, he'll see the ladder leaning up against the open window. And he'll totally panic. He'll think a burglar broke into his house."

The idea made me laugh. I have a weird laugh. It sounds more like hiccupping than laughing. Whenever I laugh, my whole family starts to laugh because my laugh is so strange.

Well, actually, Mom and Dad haven't been laughing with me much lately. Maybe I've done some things that aren't funny. Maybe I've done some things I shouldn't have. That's why I had to promise to be good and stay out of trouble.

But the ladder against the open window was definitely funny. And it wasn't such a bad thing to do, right? Especially since McClatchy is the meanest, most-hated old dude in the neighborhood.

Still laughing about my joke, I turned and started down the driveway. McClatchy has a tall hedge along the bottom of his yard. It's like a wall. I guess he really wants to keep people out.

At the end of the driveway, his mailbox stood on a tilted pole. And as I passed it, I saw the trash cans in the street. The trash was bulging up under the lids — and it gave me another cool idea.

Working fast, I pulled open the mailbox, lifted the lid off a trash can — and started to stuff trash into McClatchy's mailbox.

Yes! A greasy bag of chicken bones. A crushed soup can. Some gooey yellow stuff that looked like puke. Wet newspapers. More soup cans.

I imagined McClatchy squeaking and squealing in his high voice when he opened the mailbox and found it jammed with disgusting garbage.

What a hoot.

I started to laugh again — but quickly stopped. A choking sound escaped my throat.

Whoa.

Someone watching me. *Two* people watching, half-hidden by the tall hedge.

I froze. They stood side by side, staring right at me. I knew they saw everything. *Everything.*

A chunk of moldy cheese and a clump of newspaper fell from my hands. I staggered back from the mailbox.

Caught. I was totally caught.

"Okay. You got me. I'm sorry," I called. "I'll clean it up. Right away."

I reached into the mailbox and started to pull out trash.

But the two men didn't reply. They stood staring at me. The hedge rustled in the breeze, making shadows quiver over their still faces.

"I'm cleaning it up," I called. "No problem."

It took me a few more seconds to realize they weren't people. And they weren't alive.

"Huh?" Crumpled soda cans fell from my hands and clattered to the driveway as I took a step toward them.

Lawn gnomes.

I burst out laughing when I realized what they were.

Jay, you just freaked out because you were caught by lawn gnomes!

Walking in the shadow of the tall hedge, I stepped up to them. I placed a hand on a pointed red cap and squeezed it. Solid plaster or something.

I poked the stony dude in the eyes. I pinched his hard cheeks. "How's it going, dudes? Lookin' good!"

Nearly as tall as me, they stood side by side in red vests over matching red overalls. Beneath their pointed red caps, they had shiny round faces with white beards and white mustaches.

Their eyes were big. One had brown eyes. The other had black. They had stubby, wide noses, almost like pig snouts. Their mouths were curled down in angry scowls.

Yes, angry. They looked angry. They weren't cute. They were mean looking and ugly. Their steady, cold gaze gave me a chill.

"Stop staring at me, dudes." I covered one gnome's eyes with my hand.

I had an idea. I danced back to the trash can. Then I placed a drippy soup can on the point of one gnome's red cap. And I draped a sheet of brown-stained newspaper over his partner's shoulder.

"Now you two look cool," I said.

I stepped back to the street and slammed the lid back on the trash can. Something caught my eye. Another lawn gnome standing under a tree in McClatchy's neighbor's yard.

I squinted at it for a moment. And spotted another angry-looking gnome near the neighbor's front walk. This one wore a blue cap. Its arms were straight out as if it were directing traffic.

Why do so many homes in this neighborhood have lawn gnomes?

My family moved here only three weeks ago. This was the first time I noticed them all.

I turned and gazed across the street at the Brickmans' house next door to ours. Yes. They had three lawn gnomes lined up along their driveway.

Totally weird.

I kicked a crushed soda can onto the grass. Then I moved forward and kicked it again. I stopped as a heavy shadow swept over me.

At first, I thought it was the shadow of the hedge. Or a tree.

But then I raised my eyes — and gasped.

McClatchy!

He grabbed me by the shoulders. His hands were bony hard, like skeleton hands. He lowered his red face to me and screamed in his shrill voice:

"I've been home the whole time. Watching you. What do we do with a troublemaker?"

McClatchy squeezed my shoulders in his bony hands. Then he let go of me. He was breathing hard, making whistling noises through his nose. His eyes bulged wide.

"S-sorry," I stammered.

"You're on my bad list now," McClatchy rasped. "And believe me, kid — you don't want to be on my bad list."

"Sorry," I repeated.

His eyes were on the open mailbox, jammed with trash. His shoulders shuddered. He kept making that whistling sound. Was he going to totally lose it?

I heard the scrape of footsteps. I turned toward them. "Oh, no!"

Now I was *really* in trouble. My dad came walking toward us. He had Mr. Phineas on his leash. "What's happening here?" Dad called.

Dad is tall and athletic looking. He has wavy brown hair and dark eyes and a great, gleaming smile. Mom calls him her "movie-star husband," I guess because he's kind of handsome.

He was in his workout clothes — a gray sleeveless T-shirt over gray sweatpants.

I lowered my head as he stepped up to us. Mr. Phineas sniffed furiously at the garbage that had fallen out of the can.

"Your son had better shape up," McClatchy said through clenched teeth.

I felt Dad's eyes on me. I kept my head down.

"What has Jay done?" Dad asked. "Did he spill this garbage?"

McClatchy motioned toward the house with his head. "He moved that ladder to the open window. I think he planned to sneak into my house."

Dad gasped.

"No way!" I screamed. "I just wanted you to think —"

"I'm sure Jay wouldn't break into your house," Dad told McClatchy.

"He didn't know I was home," McClatchy said. "I saw everything."

Dad put his hand on my chin and forced me to look at him. "Jay, did you plan to go into Mr. McClatchy's house?" he demanded.

I shook my head. "No way. Of course not."

He and McClatchy stared at me for a long while, as if I were some kind of lab specimen.

Dad spoke up first. "Jay hasn't been himself lately," he told McClatchy.

McClatchy just nodded. He kept rubbing his lips over his teeth, making a wet, smacky sound.

Dad picked up the soup can and dirty newspaper from the two lawn gnomes. He stuffed the garbage in the trash can. "Very sorry," he said softly. "It won't happen again. *Will* it, Jay?"

"No," I muttered.

Mr. Phineas was licking up something green and disgusting from the spilled trash. I tugged him away and pulled the green gunk from between his teeth. Then I followed Dad across the street.

He led me into the living room. "Have a seat." He pointed to the couch. Mr. Phineas had already plopped down on the rug in front of the fireplace.

I perched on the edge of the couch. "Are we going to have a serious talk now?" I said.

Dad stood above me. He frowned. "Son, tell me. Why are you acting so strange? You know you're not supposed to play tricks on the neighbors."

I smoothed my hand over the green leather arm of the couch. "Sorry, Dad," I murmured. "I . . . was just bored."

"Find things to do," Dad snapped. "I don't want you to get in any more trouble. Do you understand me?"

I nodded.

"You can spend the next five nights after dinner in your room," Dad said. "The next time, your punishment will be a lot worse."

"But, Dad —"

He shook his head angrily. Then he spun around and stomped angrily out of the living room.

Well, Jay, you messed up again.

I slumped back on the couch. I didn't want to make people angry at me. I just wanted to have some fun.

I called to Mr. Phineas to come over to me. I felt like petting him. But he wouldn't budge from his rug by the mantel. It's his favorite place.

Kayla walked into the room. "Don't tell me you're in trouble again, Jay."

"None of your business," I snapped.

She tossed back her curly red hair and sighed. "Nothing ever changes. We had to move because of you — and now you still act like a jerk in our new home."

"I already apologized," I muttered. "Maybe you could cut me some slack?"

She shrugged. "Let's go ride our bikes."

"Huh?" I climbed up off the couch.

"You heard me. Let's ride our bikes. There's a lot of stuff in this neighborhood we haven't seen yet."

"Yeah, okay," I agreed. "At least we can't get in trouble riding our bikes — right?"

Right?

I followed Kayla outside. The afternoon sun was lowering over the trees. A cool breeze ruffled my shirt.

Our bikes were leaning against the side of the house. Kayla's bike is brand-new. It's a very sleek racing bike with about a million gears. She got it for her birthday just before we moved.

My bike is a piece of junk. The handlebars have rust spots on them. And the hand brakes only work some of the time. Usually, I have to stop my bike by scraping my shoes on the pavement.

Fun, huh?

I lifted the bike off the wall and started to walk it to the driveway. But I stopped when something at the back of the house caught my eye.

"Whoa." I set the bike back and made my way along the brick wall. The sun was in my eyes. I had to squint to see.

But as I reached the space between the house and the garage, I saw the two lawn gnomes clearly. They looked a lot like the lawn gnomes in McClatchy's yard.

They both were dressed in red. Both had the funny pointed hats. Both had white beards and mustaches.

One had its elbow against the bricks and appeared to be leaning against the side of our house. His partner had one shiny white hand raised with a finger out, as if he was pointing at me.

They both gazed wide-eyed straight ahead. Their faces were frozen in blank expressions.

Without taking my eyes off them, I called to my sister. "Kayla — when did we get these lawn gnomes? Dad didn't say anything about buying lawn gnomes."

I turned to the driveway. She was already racing away, pedaling down the street.

"Hey — wait up!" I shouted. "Wait for me!" She was out of sight. I don't think she heard me.

I made a fist and knocked on a lawn gnome's shiny red cap. "Knock knock. Anyone in there?" The cap was as hard as concrete.

I wrapped my hands around its waist and tried to pick it up. But it weighed a ton. I couldn't budge it.

Why do we have to have lawn gnomes? Just to fit in with everyone else in the neighborhood?

I thought about my friends back home. All the fun we had hanging out in the woods behind the school playground. It's sad when you have to move far away and leave your friends behind.

But my family had no choice.

I climbed onto my bike and coasted down the driveway. I gazed up and down the street. No sign of Kayla. What a pal. She just rode off without me.

I glimpsed McClatchy's yard. The tree workers were back. They were sawing off a high limb near the street.

I squinted along the hedge. "Hey!" The two lawn gnomes I'd seen there a few hours ago were gone.

I turned and stared at McClatchy's front porch. Squinting into the shadows, I saw them huddled beside the porch.

Did the workers move them away from the hedge? Were these the same lawn gnomes?

Jay, who cares? Stop thinking about stupid lawn gnomes! I scolded myself.

I turned my bike and started to pedal hard. The chain was loose, and it took a few seconds for it to catch. But then I was cruising smoothly past the big old houses and wide front lawns on my block.

I rode past the school. A bunch of kids had a soccer game going. Some boys were skateboarding in the parking lot. School doesn't start for another month, so there were no cars there.

I didn't stop. Pedaling hard, I picked up speed and rolled on. Beyond the school I saw a wide empty lot with a FOR SALE sign on it. And then two rows of houses, smaller than on my block.

I turned a corner. Still no sign of Kayla. A little white dog yipped at me and chased me for half a block. I was too fast for it. Glancing around, I realized I'd never been on this block before.

The street dipped downhill. I was sailing fast — and picking up speed.

A shout made me nearly jump off my bike.

"LOOOOOOK OUT!"

I saw the boy on the bike roaring right at me. He was *rocketing*.

I tried to stop. But my brakes didn't catch.

"NO BRAKES!" I screamed — just before the crash.

5

The hard *thud* jolted my body. My hands flew off the handlebars, and I went sailing into the air.

Not for long.

I came crashing down to the pavement with a scream. I landed hard on my side and the bike toppled onto me, tires still spinning.

I lay there for a long moment, gazing up at the trees. The setting sun made everything go red. I waited for the pain to sweep over me. But it didn't happen. I wasn't hurt much at all.

I heard a groan beside me. It snapped me alert. I shoved the bike off my chest and forced myself to sit up.

The other boy sat dazed on the street, rubbing one arm. His bike lay on its side beside him.

He was a big kid, dark haired, broad shouldered, very athletic looking. I guessed he was about my age. "You okay?" he asked. He had a gruff, hoarse voice.

"Yeah. I think so," I said. "You?"

He nodded. "Yeah. Just a scrape." He narrowed his dark eyes at me. "Didn't you see me?"

"I saw you. But my brakes are bad. I couldn't stop."

He nodded again. With a groan, he climbed to his feet. He was wearing a black T-shirt and baggy, faded jeans. One sleeve of the shirt was a little ripped from our accident.

He stood his bike up and tested it. "Seems okay." He turned back to me.

"Sorry," I said. "I'm Jay. My family just moved here."

"Elliot," he said. "Remember me?"

"No way," I said. "I don't know any kids in this neighborhood."

"I live over there." He pointed to the street across from us. Little yellow-and-white houses with square front yards.

I picked up my bike and spun the chain. It was okay. The handlebars were at a weird angle. I pushed them back where they belonged.

"Want to ride to the quagmire?" Elliot asked.

I climbed onto my bike. "Quagmire? What's that?"

"Kind of a quicksand pit."

"Cool," I said. "Is it near here?"

He motioned with his hand. "This way." He took off pedaling, and I followed him.

He made a sharp turn onto the next street. My handlebars were loose, but I managed to keep up with him.

Tall trees cast shade over the street. We rode side by side, pedaling in a steady rhythm. Elliot rode no-hands for a while.

"What's this neighborhood called?" I asked.

He shrugged. "Beats me. It's just a bunch of houses."

Then I saw two lawn gnomes in the shade of a fat tree trunk. They leaned into the tree, as if trying to hide in the shadows. In the next yard, I saw a red-costumed gnome sitting on a white rock.

I turned to Elliot. "Hey — what's up with all the lawn gnomes?" I asked.

He shrugged again. "Oh, you know." He started to pedal harder. I forced my bike to try to keep up with him.

We raced right down the middle of the street. The houses on both sides of us became a blur. We were really zooming when the quagmire came into view.

The street ended. Beyond it, I saw what looked like a wide, flat orange lake.

Elliot pressed his brakes. His bike squealed and slid to a stop at the end of the street.

I squeezed my brakes. They didn't catch. *Not again!* I squeezed harder. *No.*

I opened my mouth in a cry as my bike sailed

over the edge of the big lake. I flew several feet — and landed with a loud *plop*.

Orange gunk rose up like ocean waves on both sides of my bike.

Quicksand! I thought. *Quicksand!*

It tugged me down . . . down. My bike and I . . . we were sinking fast.

"Ohhhh . . ." A terrified moan escaped my throat.

The orange gunk was thicker than wet sand. And cold.

Sinking fast, my bike tilted hard to the left, and I started to fall off.

My hands flew from the handlebars, and I fell off the seat backward — into the goo.

I slapped the surface hard, struggling to stay on top of it. The thick sandy goo swam up to my waist. My bike was disappearing. I could see only the handlebars now.

"OWWW!" I screamed as something bit my left ankle. I felt another bite, on my other leg. Another bite.

There are creatures down below.

Snakes? Killer fish?

"OWWWWW!" They were snapping hard. Biting right through my jeans.

I tried to squirm away, but my legs were trapped under the gunk. I sank another few inches.

My heart pounding in panic, I spun around — and saw Elliot jump off his bike. He came running toward the quagmire.

Stretching out his arms, he dove toward me. He made a wild grab for my arms. Missed. And landed facedown in the muck with a sickening *splash*.

I gaped in horror as he started to sink under the surface.

"Elliot — raise your head! Pick up your head!"

No. He thrashed and kicked. But it only made him sink faster.

In seconds, he disappeared into the orange sand.

"Pick up your head! Elliot!" I screamed in a high, shrill panic. "Elliot — please!"

But he was gone. Gone. I stared down at the muck. Not even a ripple where he had sunk.

"Nooooo!" I cried out. And I leaned forward . . . forced myself to move through the muck . . . reached out my arms . . . stretched my arms over the surface.

And with a burst of strength, I bent down — and plunged both hands into the wet sand. Deeper. Until I felt something.

Yes. Elliot's head. I grabbed his head with both hands — and tugged.

Panting hard, I tugged with all my might. I pulled him by his hair. Pulled hard. Pulled his head up over the surface.

His eyes were closed. He made a choking sound. His mouth opened and he spewed an orange spray of thick gunk.

"Elliot? Elliot?" Without realizing it, I kept repeating his name.

He opened his eyes. He shook his head. His hair was thick with the orange sand. He had it caked in his nose.

"I . . . I'm okay," he said in a hoarse whisper.

26

He shook his head again. He coughed up some more gunk.

I grabbed him under the shoulders and pulled hard. He came sliding up higher. We put our hands around each other's waists. Working together, we struggled to the edge of the quagmire.

We dove onto the small patch of grass at the end of the street. We lay there for a couple of minutes, breathing, not speaking. Then we slowly climbed to our feet. It felt so awesome to stand on solid ground again.

I started to wipe the gobs of wet sand off. But I stopped when I saw the legs of my jeans. They were covered with rips and tears and bite marks.

Something caught my eye. I turned back toward the quagmire. I saw two large fish — fish with teeth and wide fins and *legs* — leap up from the sand.

I slapped Elliot on the shoulder. "Look."

Another pale green fish jumped over the surface. It had froglike legs and jagged, spiky teeth.

"I . . . never saw a fish like that," I stammered. "Why didn't you tell me this place is *dangerous*?"

Elliot wiped sand from his hair. "I didn't tell you to ride your bike right into it," he said.

"But —"

"It's a *quagmire*," he said. "Don't you know what a quagmire is? Didn't you study about them? We had it in first grade. It's in all the Beginner Geography classes."

"Huh? Not in mine!" I exclaimed. "And those gross biting fish. They kept biting and —"

I stopped as a dark shadow rolled quickly over me.

I raised my eyes and saw a *huge* creature overhead. Bigger than a swan. Black with big outstretched wings. It lowered its narrow head as it came diving down at us.

"Look out!" I cried.

"Duck!" Elliot screamed. "Hit the ground!"

I dropped flat onto my stomach and covered my head.

I felt a strong whoosh of wind as the huge bird-creature swooped over us.

Twisting my neck, I glanced up. There were *two* of them. Enormous birds. Flapping noisily above Elliot and me, preparing to dive again.

"Get flat! Get flat!" Elliot cried in a hoarse whisper.

"What are they?" I cried.

"They're Buzzard Hawks."

"Huh? They're so huge. They —"

"Get flat," he ordered. "As flat as you can."

"Why?" I demanded.

"Because they're blind."

I heard them squawking angrily above us. Their shadows rolled over us again. "Buzzard Hawks are blind?"

"They can't see, but they can smell you," Elliot whispered. "They can smell fear."

29

We both were spread out on our stomachs. I buried my face in the grass. I held my breath as I heard the enormous creatures swoop down on us again.

"Ohhhhh." I couldn't help it. I let out a moan as I felt sharp talons scrape down the back of my shirt. Pain shot through my whole body. I started to curl into a ball.

"Don't move," Elliot warned. I felt his hand on my shoulder. "They haven't smelled us down here yet. If they did . . ."

He didn't finish. The birds made another dive. I buried my face in the dirt and held my breath. Every muscle in my body tightened.

Another whoosh of wind swept over me as the birds swooped inches over us. It took only a second or two, but it seemed like an hour. Frozen in fright, I didn't move. I felt the wind off their wings, then silence.

After a long while, I slowly, carefully, lifted my head. *Yes!* The Buzzard Hawks had flown away.

I stood up, but my legs were so shaky, I could barely balance myself. "Close one," I said.

Elliot nodded. His eyes were still wide with fright. "They must have heard us when we were in the quagmire. Dangerous birds. Their claws are deadly. I mean really."

"You mean they'd claw us?" I asked.

"Claw us, then *eat* us," Elliot replied. "They're meat eaters."

I shuddered. "Let's get out of here. I don't like this place."

Elliot started to his bike. "It's not bad if you keep alert."

"Keep alert?" I shouted. "How can you keep alert against fish that chew your jeans off and birds that can rip you to pieces?"

He didn't answer. He picked up his bike and climbed onto it.

"I'm in trouble," I murmured. "I'm already in big trouble because of a thing I did to our neighbor. And now I've lost my bike. And *no way* Mom and Dad will believe me if I tell them it's at the bottom of a quagmire."

"But it's the truth," Elliot said. "I could back up your story. They'll believe me."

"Maybe," I said.

As I walked home, Elliot rode beside me, circling me, riding up a ways, then back. I didn't want to think about how we almost drowned in the quagmire. I didn't want to think about *anything* that happened there.

So I decided to count lawn gnomes as I walked. They were perched on every lawn, posted near driveways, leaning against tree trunks. Ugly little bearded fellows in red outfits and those funny caps.

Totally weird.

I counted thirty-two of them, and I was still a few blocks from home. Most of them stared straight out to the street, as if they were watching, watching us pass by with their big, blank painted eyes.

"In my old neighborhood, *no one* had lawn gnomes," I told Elliot. "We thought they were too ugly to put on front lawns. I don't get it. Really. Why are these stupid little men everywhere I look?"

He spun his bike around. "I've got to go. This is my street." He pointed. "Do you know the rest of the way?"

I nodded. "Yeah. Sure."

"Well, see you around," he said. "Thanks for saving my life." He started to pedal away. "Sorry about your bike," he called.

"Yeah. Me, too," I said. I watched him ride down the street. He turned into the driveway of a little yellow-and-white house at the end of the block.

I turned and started walking slowly toward my house. The sun was nearly down. The sky was streaked with red.

Lawn gnomes stared at me from front yards as I passed. But I didn't feel like counting anymore.

I was worried about my lost bike. I'd promised my parents I'd be more responsible in our new neighborhood. And here I was, coming home without my bike.

I sighed. *Maybe they won't notice,* I told myself.

I turned at my house and walked up the front lawn. To my surprise, two lawn gnomes stood on the front porch.

Who moved them? I wondered.

I climbed onto the porch, stepped past the ugly little gnomes, and started to open the front door.

"Jay — where is your bike?" one of them demanded.

I gasped. I raised my eyes. And saw my dad on the other side of the screen door.

The lawn gnome didn't speak to me. Of *course* not. It was Dad. "Where's your bike?" he repeated.

"Uh . . . well . . . It's a long story," I murmured.

He held open the door and I slumped into the house. "Did you lose it?" he demanded.

"Kinda," I said. "It's at the bottom of a quagmire."

He squinted at me. He didn't look happy.

"I knew you wouldn't believe me," I said.

Dad sighed. "I don't know *what* to believe. I don't want to keep punishing you. But, Jay, you promised —"

"Dad, what's up with all the lawn gnomes?" I asked. "Those two on the porch. And in every yard. And —"

"You know," Dad said.

Mom called from the kitchen. "Hey, you two — supper is almost ready. Time to eat."

34

Dad turned and strode to the kitchen. "Coming, dear."

I hurried upstairs to wash up. I could smell myself. I smelled like a swamp. I thought about sinking in that sandy orange goo, and it made me shudder.

I wasn't sure I liked my new neighborhood. In two words, it was dangerous and creepy.

Of course, I had no idea how creepy it really was.

The next afternoon, I stayed in my room. Sunlight poured in through my window, and a warm breeze ruffled the curtains. But I didn't feel like going outside.

I set up my test tubes and glass beakers on my lab table. Then I arranged my chemical bottles.

I've always been a science freak. I love taking chemicals at random, mixing them together, and seeing the results. It's relaxing and exciting at the same time.

I studied the brown glass bottles, trying to decide what kind of mixture to create. I poured a little bit of a bright orange chemical I made into a large beaker. Then I added just a drip of hydrogen peroxide.

It made a soft hissing sound, and it smelled sharp and bitter.

I stirred in a few teaspoons of magnesium. But it didn't seem to do anything at all.

When my family moved here three weeks ago, my parents tried to stop me from bringing my chemistry set. I mean, we had to move because of all the trouble I caused with my chemicals.

And we all wanted a clean start. No one in our new town knew about what I had done. Mom and Dad wanted to make sure it never happened again.

But my chemicals are just too important to me. How could I leave them behind?

Working with chemicals and learning about science isn't just a hobby with me. It's what I care about more than anything in the world. Maybe someday I'll be a famous scientist, and I'll create something totally terrific.

I screamed and cried and begged and pleaded. But they said no. So, I had no choice. I hid my chemistry set in a carton of blankets and sneaked it into the house.

I raised a test tube of a new acid I discovered and I tilted it into my mixing beaker. The acid made the liquid inside start to bubble and fizz.

"Hey, what's up?"

Kayla walked into the room. She startled me. I almost dropped the tube of acid.

"Don't you ever knock?"

She ignored my question and stepped up to the lab table. "Eww, that stinks. What are you doing?"

I snickered. "I'm mixing up a special drink for McClatchy."

Kayla didn't laugh. "Stop it, Jay. That's not funny. Stop thinking about pranks and mean tricks to play on people."

I held out the fizzing beaker. "Take a sip. See if it's ready."

She stepped back. "You're really being stupid. You know that?"

I didn't answer. I poured a little more acid in the beaker and watched it bubble.

But Kayla wasn't finished scolding me. "I can't believe you're mixing chemicals again. You promised Mom and Dad," she said. "You promised them you've changed. You said you'd be responsible from now on."

"So?" I shot back.

"So you got caught stuffing McClatchy's mailbox with garbage, and you lost your bike."

"That wasn't my fault," I said.

"Go ahead. Do something responsible," she said. "Do something to impress Mom and Dad."

I set the test tube back in its holder. "Like what?"

Kayla thought for a moment. "Go take Mr. Phineas on his afternoon walk. Do it before they ask you to do it."

"Good idea," I said. "I'll do it." I started to close the lids on the chemical bottles. "Kayla, do you want to come with me?"

She shook her head. "Too boring." She turned and ran from the room.

A few minutes later, I snapped the leash on Mr. Phineas, and we set off walking down the front lawn. "Mr. Phineas, stop pulling," I cried. "Stop it. You're pulling the leash from my hand." The dog was pulling like crazy. Excited to be outside, I guess.

"Mr. Phineas — stop! Mr. Phineas — slow down, boy!"

To my surprise, the two lawn gnomes had been moved from the front porch. Now they were at the bottom of the driveway.

Across the street, McClatchy's two lawn gnomes stood at the curb. The four bearded gnomes appeared to be having a staring match!

Who keeps moving them around? I wondered.

And more important, *why?*

What a mystery. So far, I couldn't get anyone to answer my questions about them.

More gnomes stared at us from front yards as Mr. Phineas pulled me down the street. At one house, I saw *five* of them standing in a circle. The gnomes' arms were outstretched. It looked like they were holding hands.

Totally weird.

"Hey — stop!" I let out a cry as Mr. Phineas took off. I saw a squirrel half a block away. "No — stop! *Stop!*"

The leash flew out of my hand. Barking his head off, the big dog went *tearing* down the middle of the street. The squirrel froze for a moment, then turned and scampered away.

"Mr. Phineas! Come back! Come back!"

In a panic, I stumbled after him, shouting, begging him to stop his hunt. But nothing can stop Mr. Phineas when he spots a squirrel.

"Mr. Phineas! Stop! Come back!"

The leash whipped along the pavement behind him as he ran. I didn't see the squirrel anywhere. It had probably climbed a tree.

But the dog didn't slow down.

"Mr. Phineas — *please*!"

And then I saw a dark green car turn onto the street. And I staggered to a stop, my body frozen in horror.

"No! Noooo! Mr. Phineas — LOOK OUT!"

I shut my eyes and listened to the squeal of tires.

A deafening crash made me jump. I heard a man scream.

It forced me to open my eyes. I saw the green car, its front fender crushed against a light pole.

Mr. Phineas?

I heard his bark. And saw him running down the middle of the street, into the next block.

The car had missed him. The big dog didn't even stop running.

The passenger door swung open. A man in a dark suit staggered out, shaking his head. He gripped the top of the car, as if holding himself up.

"S-sorry," I stammered as I ran past.

He called out. But I kept running. I had to catch Mr. Phineas before he caused another accident.

I took the dog out to prove how responsible I was. And now the dog caused an accident and ran away. I knew I was in major trouble.

And guess what? It got worse.

"Mr. Phineas! Mr. Phineas!" I screamed at the dog.

He finally slowed down. I guess he saw that the squirrel had escaped and he was chasing nothing.

"Stop! Stop!" I was running hard, still half a block behind him.

I gasped as a dark shadow rolled over me. I heard flapping wings. Then another shadow swept past.

It happened so fast, I didn't have a chance to scream or do anything.

Gasping for breath, I stood and watched as two enormous Buzzard Hawks shot down from the sky. They swooped onto Mr. Phineas, squawking loudly, their huge black wings beating the air.

The big dog swung his head around. Snarling, he bared his teeth and tried to snap at them.

But the birds were too big, too powerful.

Gripped with terror, I watched as they dug their talons into the fur on his back. They raised their heads and flapped their wings furiously.

And started to lift Mr. Phineas off the ground.

"Noooo!" A howl burst from deep inside me.

The Buzzard Hawks squawked and flapped. Mr. Phineas swung his head back and forth, struggling to free himself.

They lifted him a foot off the ground. I took a running leap. Dove forward. Stretched out my arms to grab him away from them.

Stretched . . . stretched . . .

And missed.

I landed hard on the pavement. Skidded several feet on my stomach.

It knocked my breath out. I wheezed and choked and struggled to force air into my lungs.

And watched as the screaming, squawking monster birds flew off with Mr. Phineas.

Sucking in deep breaths of air, I forced myself to my feet. The huge birds cast wide shadows on the street as they flew away with my dog. The poor guy let out a howl of fright.

My sneakers slapped the pavement as I ran after the birds. They were high above me, flapping their long black wings, and pulling themselves higher.

"Ohh." I stumbled over something. A large glass soda bottle. It rolled away from me toward the curb.

Without stopping to think about it, I bent down and grabbed the bottle. I didn't have time to take aim or plan my throw. With a loud groan, I *heaved* the bottle into the air. Heaved it at the squawking birds.

I heard a hard *thump*.

A Buzzard Hawk screamed.

The birds flew apart. And Mr. Phineas came sailing down.

My heart did a flip-flop in my chest. I reached out my arms. He was falling fast. The dog's legs were thrashing the air. His tail tucked between his legs. Too terrified to make a sound.

I had to catch him. I had to —

"OWWW!" I cried out in pain as he crashed into my arms like a meteorite falling to the ground. I fell onto my back and he landed on my chest. In the sky, I saw the two Buzzard Hawks floating away.

"Mr. Phineas — stop it! Come on, boy — stop!" Still on top of me, the big jerk began licking my face. "Please — stop!"

I suddenly remembered the driver. The green car. The accident.

In my attempt to rescue Mr. Phineas, I'd forgotten all about him. I grabbed the dog's leash and, wrapping the end around my hand, raced back.

"This is *your* fault, Mr. Phineas," I scolded as we ran.

The dog wagged his tail a little harder. He didn't understand.

I found the man in the dark suit still standing by the light pole. He had short brown hair parted in the middle, brown eyes, a small mustache, and a pointed chin. He was muttering to himself as he walked in a circle around the pole and his wrecked car.

He didn't see me until I called out to him. "Are you okay?"

He stopped circling and stared at me. "Malfunction," he shouted in a high, shrill voice. "Malfunction."

"I . . . don't understand," I said. I stepped closer. Mr. Phineas sniffed the light pole. "Are you okay?" I repeated.

"Malfunction," the man said. "Malfunction."

Oh, no. He must have hit his head.

He just kept repeating that word. His eyes were glassy. He had no expression on his face at all.

"Malfunction. Malfunction. Malfunction."

I didn't know what to do. He probably had a concussion or something. I glanced all around. No one else in sight.

"Malfunction. Malfunction."

"I . . . I'll get help," I stammered. I motioned with both hands. "Stay here, okay? Do you want to sit down? I'm going to call for help."

"Malfunction. Malfunction." His fingers were all moving at once, tapping the sides of his suit pants. "Malfunction."

I tugged Mr. Phineas away from the light pole. My plan was to hurry to the nearest house and ask them to call 911. Mr. Phineas tugged back. He wasn't finished sniffing the pole.

I gave a hard yank on the leash and started to jog toward the small, square redbrick house on the corner.

"Malfunction. Malfunction."

I glanced back and saw the poor man circling his car again. Muttering that word over and over.

I'm in major trouble. I've never been in trouble this bad.

Oh, well. Actually, I have. But this is pretty bad.

I didn't see the car coming from behind until it pulled to a stop across the street from me. "Is there a problem here?"

The voice startled me. I looked over and saw two blue-uniformed police officers inside a black-and-white patrol car.

I let out a sigh. "Oh, thank goodness," I said. "Th-there's been an accident." I pointed.

The two officers climbed quickly out of their car. They left the doors open and started toward me.

I hurried back to the man circling the light pole. "Malfunction. Malfunction."

I turned to the two cops. "It . . . it wasn't my fault. Really," I stammered.

But their eyes narrowed as they came at me. Their shoulders tensed. They lowered their hands over their holsters. And they stared coldly at me as they moved in.

"Hey —" I gasped. "What are you going to *do*?"

I staggered back until I bumped into the green car.

Eyes narrowed coldly, the two cops kept coming.

"Wait. Please —" I pleaded.

To my surprise, they walked right past me. They strode up to the man circling the light pole.

"Malfunction," he said. "Malfunction."

"Yeah, we know," one of the cops said.

They both grabbed the man. Each cop took a shoulder.

Looking confused, the man swung his head from side to side. "Malfunction. Malfunction."

The cops pushed him quickly to the patrol car. The man made no attempt to resist. He just kept moving his head back and forth and repeating the one word.

They pushed him into the backseat of the car and slammed the door. A few seconds later, the car started up and they roared away.

I stood there, stunned. Mr. Phineas tugged at his leash. He sniffed the grass beside the damaged car. I could still hear the roar of the patrol car as it sped down the street.

"I'm in so much trouble," I told the dog. "I was just trying to be responsible. And now look." I shook my head sadly.

Mr. Phineas gazed up at me for a moment. Then he went back to his sniffing.

That poor man, I thought. *He's totally messed up.*

I promised I wouldn't get in trouble when we moved here. And now I was probably in the worst trouble of my life.

I started to walk Mr. Phineas home. The sun was nearly down. We walked through long shadows.

I couldn't stop thinking about the accident. Mr. Phineas loped along slowly, tired from his adventure.

We passed a group of lawn gnomes standing at the bottom of a wide lawn. They all had sick smiles on their faces. As if they knew what had happened to me and were grinning merrily about it.

Don't let your imagination run away with you, Jay, I scolded myself. *They are ugly little men molded out of plaster. Don't get crazy just because they have smiles painted on their faces.*

Mr. Phineas led the way onto our block. He started to pull on the leash. I guess he was eager to get home and have his dinner.

A feeling of heavy dread fell over me. My stomach started to churn. I knew I had to tell my parents about the accident as soon as I got home.

We passed another group of grinning lawn gnomes. I had my head down. My brain was spinning.

Suddenly, I felt Mr. Phineas tug hard at his leash. I looked up and saw a fat gray cat slither across the street.

Mr. Phineas let out a fierce bark — and took off after the cat. The leash flew out of my hand. Barking ferociously, the big dog galloped down the street.

"Oh, noooo!" I wailed. "Not again!"

The street was empty. No cars coming toward us. But Mr. Phineas turned suddenly and, barking his head off, roared past a tall hedge and into a front yard.

It took me a few seconds to recognize the house. And then I screamed my lungs out: "No! Mr. Phineas — NO! Not McClatchy's yard! No! Not McClatchy!"

I chased after the big dog, but *no way* could I catch him. Four legs are always faster than two — especially when they're on a golden Lab.

He galloped right between two lawn gnomes standing beside the front walk. And finally stopped on McClatchy's front porch.

"No! Get away!" I shouted, running up the middle of the yard. "Mr. Phineas — move! Get off the porch!"

I was just a few feet away when I realized the dog wasn't standing right. He had hunched his whole body. His head was down.

A deep groan escaped Mr. Phineas's throat. He tightened his body even more. His tail was tucked tightly between his legs.

I recognized that pose. The dog was going to be sick.

I couldn't get there in time. I stood and watched as Mr. Phineas started to vomit. Groaning and moaning, he choked up big hunks of puke.

His whole body heaved and shook as he vomited up a messy pile.

Guess where? Yes. Right in front of McClatchy's front door.

"Mr. Phineas, come," I ordered. "Come here. Mr. Phineas — come."

The dog stood up straight and licked the vomit off his lips.

"Mr. Phineas — get away from there."

I moved forward to grab the leash — and the front door swung open. The porch light flashed on.

McClatchy squinted out at me. His expression quickly turned angry. "Hey — what's your dog doing on my front porch?" he snarled.

"I'm sorry, Mr. McClatchy," I started. "Please don't walk —"

He pulled the front door in farther and stepped out. His foot landed in the mountain of puke. It made a sick *squisssh*.

McClatchy's mouth dropped open as he slipped on the vomit. His foot slid out behind him — and he fell facedown on the porch. Vomit splashed up in a high wave.

Muttering to himself, he slipped and slid in it. Finally, he managed to pull himself to his feet.

He shook his fists in the air and screamed his lungs out for a long moment. Then he pulled back his leg — and *kicked* Mr. Phineas in the belly.

The dog uttered a *yelp*. It was a hard kick. Mr. Phineas landed on his feet in front of me, whimpering softly.

McClatchy stood glaring at me, hands on his hips.

"Hey!" I shouted angrily. "You can't kick my dog!"

McClatchy stuck his jaw out. "I just did. What are you going to do about it, kid?"

I stared back at him. I was too angry to speak. My hands were balled into tight fists. My chest felt about to explode.

"Well? What are you going to do about it?" McClatchy repeated.

I'll think of something, I told myself. *Don't worry, McClatchy. I'll think of something.*

That night, I was up in my room, moving my chemical bottles around on the lab table. I was too angry and upset to work with my chemistry set. But it felt good to move the bottles around.

I didn't tell my parents about the car accident. I was trying to think of a *good* way to give them the news.

Kayla sat on the edge of my bed, resting her head in her hands. "You have to calm down," she said. "You're totally losing it."

"I'm not losing it," I said. "Mr. Phineas has to be avenged."

"You have to be careful," Kayla warned.

"I can't be careful," I told her. "I have to teach McClatchy a lesson. He can't just kick someone's dog because they puke on his porch."

Kayla locked her eyes on me. "You're looking for trouble."

I banged a bottle on the table. "*McClatchy* is the one looking for trouble."

She sighed and stood up. She brushed her red hair back. "So what do you plan to do?"

"I . . . don't know," I replied. "I'm going to sneak out. I'm going over to McClatchy's house. But I don't know what I'll do when I get there."

She shook her head. "Jay, you know you're not allowed to go out after dinner."

"Tell someone who cares," I said.

She stomped her foot and strode out of the room.

"Are you going to tell on me?" I shouted.

She didn't answer.

I went to the window and stared down at the street. It was a clear, still night. The trees didn't move. The sky was a deep purple. Streetlights sent a pale yellow glow over McClatchy's tall hedge at the curb.

Suddenly, I knew what I would do to get my revenge. I chuckled to myself. Sure, it was mean. It was *very* mean.

But McClatchy deserved it. He had to be taught a lesson. I had to stand up for Mr. Phineas and all dogs everywhere.

My head buzzed with excitement. My hands felt clammy. I could feel my heartbeats fluttering in my chest.

Yes. Yes. This was mean . . . but *perfect*.

I crossed the room to my bookshelf and bent down to the bottom shelf. I found the old book under a pile of magazines. It was a book I'd found in the library back home.

It was yellowed and dust smeared, and the pages were cracked. But I stole it from the library because it was the most amazing chemistry book ever written.

The faded title on the front of the book read *Chemycal Magyk*. There was no author name.

Maybe the author wanted to keep hidden. Because the instructions in the book were dangerous and frightening.

The chemical mixtures were like witchcraft or sorcery. Not science.

The formulas and mixtures could do horrible things to people. Change people into monsters. Make them grow fur or fangs. Or shrink them to the size of insects.

It was crazy. It was wild. It seemed impossible. But the mysterious author claimed that anyone could make these potions out of simple chemicals. I'd buried the book on the bottom of my shelf because it scared me a little.

But now it was time to drag it out and use it. McClatchy asked for it. And I knew exactly which mixture I wanted to make.

My hands trembled as I gathered the ingredients. I was nervous and frightened and excited all at the same time.

And as I began to measure and pour, a smile crossed my face.

McClatchy, you are doomed. . . .

I stepped out into the night. I crossed the street and walked up the sloping lawn to McClatchy's front stoop.

Holding the glass bottle in one hand, I knocked on the front door with the other.

McClatchy was surprised to see me. He greeted me with a cold sneer. "What are *you* doing here?"

"I came to apologize," I said softly. I flashed him my most sincere look. "I feel so bad about what happened."

He blinked. "Apologize?"

I nodded. "Can I come in?" I held up the bottle with its dark liquid. "I brought you a cold drink."

He squinted at me, studying me. Then he slowly opened the screen door.

I stepped into his front room. The room was dimly lit. The furniture was all black and gray. Weird music played. It sounded like a lot of whistles tooting at once.

I handed him the bottle. "Try this," I said. "It's a cold drink for you. My way of saying sorry."

He took the bottle and sniffed it. "Smells good."

"I hope you like it," I said. "I really do want to apologize. I swear things will be different from now on."

I watched him take a sip of my liquid mixture. He seemed to like it. He took a long drink. Then he tilted the bottle and drank it all down.

"Good, right?" I said.

He licked his lips. Then he blinked his eyes several times.

"Did you enjoy it?" I asked.

"*Woof woof,*" he said.

"Good," I replied.

"*Woof woof rrrrufff wooof,*" McClatchy barked.

"Good boy. That's a good boy," I said. I patted him on the head.

His eyes bulged and his eyebrows rose up high on his head. "*Woof woof?*"

"Yes," I said. "Yes, you get it, McClatchy, boy. You're a dog now. My special drink turned you into a dog."

"*Woof woof.*" He nodded. He was definitely catching on.

"Why don't you get down on all fours?" I said. "Now that you're a dog, you have to learn to walk like a dog."

"*Woof?*" He stared at me for a long moment. Then he lowered himself to the floor.

"Now, stand still," I said. "Don't move."

"Woof?"

"I'm going to kick you across the room."

The surprised look on his face made me laugh. The laughter just tumbled out of me. I couldn't stop. I laughed and laughed.

I stopped when a loud voice behind me shouted, "Jay? What are you doing? What's so funny?"

16

I blinked. I was standing in my bedroom. Dad filled the doorway.

He squinted at me. "I heard you laughing all the way downstairs. What's so funny?"

I shrugged. "Nothing," I said. "Just day-dreaming."

"Must have been a funny daydream," Dad said.

"It was," I answered.

It was a very funny daydream. But too bad. Only a daydream.

Dad waved and went back downstairs.

I sat down on my bed and thought hard. I didn't know what I wanted to do to get my revenge on McClatchy. I didn't have any weird spell book. That was just something my crazy brain dreamed up.

But I knew I had to do something.

I'm going over there. Maybe I'll think of something good when I get there.

I waited awhile. I didn't want Mom or Dad to catch me. I knew I wasn't allowed out at night.

But I had to risk it. I wouldn't be able to sleep if I didn't.

So after a while, I crept down the stairs, careful not to make the steps squeak. I peeked into the living room. Dad had fallen asleep with a magazine on his lap. I didn't see Mom.

I turned and tiptoed to the kitchen. Mr. Phineas was curled up under the breakfast table. He was sound asleep, snoring noisily.

I slipped past him and stepped out the back door. I closed it carefully, silently. I took a deep breath of the cool, crisp night air.

My whole body tingled. I knew I was excited. My heart was thudding in my chest — this time for real.

I turned and, pressing against the wall along the side of the house, made my way to the street. I could see the tall hedge and beyond it, the dark shape of McClatchy's house.

What was I going to do there? What was I going to do to McClatchy?

I still didn't know. I just knew I wanted to do something *really bad*.

I stopped at the hedge. My legs suddenly felt weak and rubbery. I was breathing noisily, my chest heaving up and down.

I held my breath when I heard a flapping sound overhead. Beating wings. Was it a bat? A Buzzard Hawk?

I pressed my back into the prickly hedge and waited for it to fly away. Then I turned toward McClatchy's house. Pitch-black. Not a light on anywhere.

The front yard stretched in shades of black and gray.

I should have brought a flashlight. I can't see a thing.

My sneakers scraped the driveway as I began to walk toward the house.

I still had no idea what I planned to do.

I'm not really a bad kid. Sure, I got in a lot of trouble in the old neighborhood. And today.

But I don't *try* to be bad. I mean, I'm not *evil* or anything.

But tonight I knew I was doing the right thing. This man had kicked my dog. Kicked him really hard. And he deserved to be punished for it.

Staring up at the dark house, I made my way step by step up the driveway, walking slowly, carefully.

I didn't see the man standing in front of me until I bumped right into him.

"Oh!" I uttered a startled cry. "I'm sorry!"

He didn't speak. He didn't move at all.

"I . . . I didn't mean to bump you," I stammered. But then, in the pale light from a streetlamp at the curb, I saw that it wasn't a man at all. It was a lawn gnome.

How did it get in the middle of McClatchy's driveway?

I squinted hard at it. The little man's eyes appeared to glow in the dim light. His pointed hat was tilted on his head. His mouth was turned down in an angry scowl.

I glanced around. McClatchy had two lawn gnomes. I didn't see the other one. Maybe it was hidden in the blackness under the tall hedge.

I put my hand on the gnome's hat and squeezed the top. To my surprise, the hat felt *soft* — not hard as plaster.

Suddenly, I had an idea.

I pulled a black marker from my jeans pocket. I had brought it along in case I found something to mark up. And now I had found it — this lawn gnome.

I giggled to myself. I pulled the top off the marker.

My plan was to paint the dude's white mustache. Make it bigger and black. And make his eyes cross. And blacken a few of his front teeth.

This would definitely make McClatchy angry. If I could find the other gnome, I'd mark him up, too.

Then maybe I could break off the gnomes' stupid hats. I'd break off their pointy hats and leave them on the ground in front of them.

That idea made me giggle again.

If McClatchy wants to mess with my dog, it's only fair that I mess with his lawn gnomes.

I raised the marker and moved it to the gnome's mustache.

"I wouldn't do that if I were you!" the gnome rasped. Its hand shot up and grabbed me by the throat.

"Unnnnh." I started to choke as a sharp pain swept down my neck.

The gnome's fingers were bone hard. He tightened his grip, squeezing my throat.

I couldn't breathe. I tried to squirm away. But he clamped his hand even tighter. He had amazing strength for such a little creature.

I thrashed my arms. Tried to punch him. But he held me out in front of him, choking me . . . choking me.

His dark eyes glowed with excitement. His whole face was clenched tight from his effort to hold me in place.

Please . . .

I could feel my face grow hot. I struggled to hit him, but my arms felt weak. I was going limp.

No air. No air. The pain was intense.

I shut my eyes. To my surprise, the pain suddenly grew lighter. The gnome let go of me.

I stumbled back and dropped to my knees.

The lawn gnome stood over me, clenching and unclenching his fist. *"Heh heh heh."* His mouth opened in a hoarse chuckle. It sounded like a chicken's cluck.

Gasping for air, I tried to rub the pain from my throat. On my knees, we were about the same height. He chuckled again, his eyes catching the light from the street.

How can this be? Lawn gnomes can't come to life.

I knew it wasn't a dream. I was in too much pain to be dreaming.

Rubbing his beard, the gnome moved toward me. Was he going to choke me again?

I jumped to my feet. My mind whirring in panic, I spun away from him. I turned to run.

But I bumped right into the other lawn gnome. He let out an ugly grunt and wrapped his hands around my waist. His hands were hard as steel. He grunted again and tried to lift me off the ground.

Gripping me around the middle, he pressed his face against my arm as he struggled to raise me. His cheek was warm. It felt like human skin.

His breath was sour and disgusting. He uttered grunt after grunt.

"Let go!" I screamed. I brought both hands up and shoved him hard under his beard.

It caught him by surprise. His hands fell away.

I gave him another hard shove. It sent him toppling into his partner.

They both made awkward grabs for me. But I dodged away. And then I ran, faster than I'd ever run.

My feet slid on McClatchy's lawn, and then pounded the driveway. I ran through the blackness of the night. Not seeing anything. Not thinking. Just moving on fear and shock.

I crossed the street, panting hard. I started up my front lawn.

I could hear them behind me, chattering as they chased after me. I heard the clatter of their boots on the pavement. Then the pounding of footsteps as they ran over the grass.

I froze in panic. Then forced myself to move.

I leaped onto my front porch. If I could only get through the front door, into the house, I'd be safe.

I grabbed the door handle — then screamed in horror.

Two other lawn gnomes came charging at me from either side of the porch. They dove at me, lowering their shoulders, trying to tackle me around the knees.

With a cry, I leaped back. They thudded hard against each other, cracking heads.

"Oh, nooo!"

I uttered a cry as I saw McClatchy's gnomes running up my front lawn. And two more gnomes from my other neighbor. And a whole bunch of them from down the street.

All running. All grunting. All heading for me.

Their pointed caps tilted toward me as they ran. Their hands were outstretched, ready to grab me.

They chattered and whistled and cried out in a language I never heard before. Like the chatter of birds.

I spun away. Started to the right. No. More gnomes closing in on me. With another cry, I spun to the left.

No escape. No escape from them.

I was trapped. They formed a circle around me — a dozen of them. No — more! The circle tightened. Chattering and whistling, the gnomes closed in on me.

"Get away!" I screamed. "Stay away from me, you little freaks!"

The gnomes ignored my screams. They tightened the circle till I could barely breathe. Then two lawn gnomes grabbed my arms and twisted them back.

I couldn't move. For such little guys, they were incredibly strong.

The gnomes from McClatchy's yard strode up to me. In the dim light, I saw that one of them held something behind his back.

"Wh-what is that?" I stammered. "What are you going to do?"

A cold smile spread over his face as he moved closer. His putrid breath floated over me. It almost made me gag.

What is he hiding behind his back? What is he going to do to me?

He giggled and raised his arm. He had the black marker in his hand.

"Stop!" I cried. "Let me go!"

But our porch gnomes held me in place, my arms tightly behind my back. McClatchy's gnome raised the marker and began to scrape it against my forehead.

I could feel the lines he drew. I knew they formed an M.

Why an M? What does that stand for?

McClatchy?

No. I guessed wrong.

"*Malfunction,*" the gnome rasped in his scratchy, high voice.

"*Malfunction,*" the gnomes all repeated.

"*Malfunction. Malfunction.*"

They giggled and bumped each other's shoulders. Like a gnome high five.

"What are you saying?" I cried. "Why are you saying that?"

They giggled some more and bumped shoulders.

With a cry, I burst forward — and broke free. I took off, running hard.

I could hear them chattering like birds and giggling behind me. I glanced back. They weren't chasing after me.

I hurled myself along the side of the house. Turned at the back and shoved open the kitchen door. Gasping, I bolted inside and slammed the door hard behind me.

I pressed my back against the kitchen door and listened. I couldn't hear them now. Were they still hanging out in my front yard? No way to tell.

My heart was pounding. I took a deep breath and held it, but that didn't help. Drops of sweat rolled down my forehead.

I pushed away from the door and strode quickly into the living room. Mom and Dad turned to me from the center of the room. They both squinted at me.

"Jay, were you outside?" Dad demanded.

"We thought you were in your room," Mom said. "You know you're not supposed to go outside after dark."

"I . . . I know," I stammered. "But —"

"I'm very disappointed in you," Dad said, shaking his head. "You promised you would follow the rules here. And instead . . ."

"Lawn gnomes!" I cried. "Listen to me. You've got to hear what happened to me!"

They glanced at each other, then turned back to me. "What's that mark on your forehead?" Mom asked. "It looks like an M."

"Please," I begged. "Listen to me. Outside, there were lawn gnomes. Dozens of them. And they came to life. Really. They chased me across the street. They put this M on my forehead."

They stared at me without moving or speaking.

"I'm not making this up," I said breathlessly. "The lawn gnomes came to life. They grabbed me. They choked me. You've *got* to believe me. I saw them. Please — believe me."

I stood there, breathing hard. My heart pounded so fast, my chest hurt.

"Of course we believe you," Dad said finally. "Of course the lawn gnomes came alive. Of course they chased you."

"What did you expect?" Mom said.

I stared at them both in disbelief.

Am I losing my mind?

Mom and Dad refused to say another word about it. They said it was too late at night to talk. I begged them to explain. But they said it could wait till morning. They ordered me up to my room.

The next morning, I hurried down to breakfast so they could explain about the lawn gnomes. But Dad gave me a half-hour lecture instead. He was angry and upset. He hardly let me get a word in.

"Jay, you promised," he said. "You know perfectly well that no one goes out at night. Yet you decided for some reason —"

"I *had* to go out," I started. "I —"

"You're not supposed to break the rules, Jay. And the rule is to stay indoors at night. But you chose not to pay any attention to it."

I lowered my head. "Yeah, you're right about that," I murmured. "But I had a good reason. Mr. McClatchy —"

Dad frowned at me. "Jay, we talked about not causing trouble with the neighbors. You promised you would stop playing jokes on people."

"But he kicked Mr. Phineas."

"I don't care what Mr. McClatchy did," Dad said. "We are talking about *you*. Are you going to obey the rules here and stop getting in trouble?" He moved his face close to mine.

I had no choice. "Yes," I said. "Yes. I promise, Dad. From now on, I'll be perfect."

I meant it, too. I didn't have my fingers crossed or anything.

I decided it might be a lot easier to be good. And it definitely would be easier to stay out of trouble.

Dad took his coffee cup into the other room. I heard a cough. I turned and saw Elliot, the kid from the quagmire, standing at the kitchen door.

"Hey," I said. I felt embarrassed. *How much did he hear? Did he hear Dad's whole lecture to me?*

"How's it going?" Elliot asked. "Did you get in trouble for losing your bike?"

I shook my head. "No. I got in trouble for something else," I said.

Maybe Elliot can tell me what's up with the lawn gnomes coming to life.

"Come up to my room," I said. I led him upstairs.

"Nice house," he said in his gruff voice.

"It's okay," I replied.

We stepped into my room. I had a lot of chemicals open and equipment strewn over my lab table. He glanced at it, then perched on the edge of my bed.

He pushed back his black hair and gazed around. He looked bigger — wider — indoors than outdoors. Like he was almost too big for my bed. He wasn't fat, just a big kid.

I pulled my tall lab stool across from him and sat down on it. "Something weird happened to me last night," I said. "Maybe you can help me."

He squinted at me. "Help you?"

"I went over to McClatchy's house," I said. I pointed out the bedroom window. "And these lawn gnomes —"

His eyes went wide. "You went outside at night? Really?"

"Well . . . yeah," I said. "And these lawn gnomes . . . they were *alive*. They grabbed me and —"

He suddenly looked away. I could see pink circles on his cheeks. He was blushing. He mumbled something, but I couldn't hear him.

"What's wrong?" I asked. "Do you know about the lawn gnomes coming alive? Tell me. You have to tell me!"

He shrugged his big shoulders. "You know," he muttered. He kept his eyes on the window.

74

"No, really," I said. "I *don't* know. Tell me. How do the gnomes come alive? They're just hunks of painted plaster, right?"

Elliot sighed. "Come on, Jay. You know the answer. Why are you doing this?"

"I don't know the answer," I said. "I need you to tell me. They grabbed me, Elliot. It was totally scary. They took a marker and made a big M on my forehead."

"Oh, wow," Elliot muttered.

"They kept repeating this word. *Malfunction. Malfunction.* Do you know what that means?"

He finally turned his eyes to me. "No," he said. "No. What does it mean?"

"I'm asking *you*!" I cried. "Why can't you help me? Listen. Mr. Phineas got free and caused a car crash. And the driver of the car kept saying the same word. *Malfunction. Malfunction.* What does it mean? Why was he doing that?"

"Beats me," Elliot said.

He jumped to his feet and strode to the lab table. He gazed over the table and picked up a test tube. "You're into science?"

I could see he wasn't going to help me. I followed him to the table. "I like to experiment with chemicals," I told him. "Create different mixtures and see how the chemicals react. And sometimes I come up with things. You know. Inventions."

He set the test tube down carefully. "Inventions?"

I nodded. "I'll show you," I said.

I pulled up the thing I'd been working on. I handed it to him.

He rolled it around in his hand. "It's a candle?"

"It looks like a candle," I said. I took it back from him. "But I call it a light-stick. See, you don't need a match to light it up. I treated it with chemicals. You just blow on the end to light it, then blow once more to put it out."

I raised the light-stick between us, sucked in a deep breath, and blew on it. Quickly, I turned my eyes away. I knew how bright the flash would be.

It made a FIZZZZZ sound, then a POP. A bright yellow flame exploded from the end of the stick. The flame surrounded both of us in bright light.

Elliot's eyes bulged. He uttered a sharp cry. And dropped to the floor with a groan. His head bounced on the floor. He lay sprawled on his back, eyes shut, not moving.

I let out a startled gasp. Was it too bright for him? I blew out the light-stick. Then I whirled around the side of the table and dropped to my knees beside him.

Oh, no! What have I done?

21

"Elliot? Elliot?" I repeated his name. "What happened? Are you okay? Can you hear me?"

He opened his eyes. A smile spread over his face. "Just joking," he said.

He sat up. "Ha-ha. You looked totally freaked."

I swallowed. My mouth was dry as cotton. "No way," I lied. "I knew you were faking. I knew it was a dumb joke."

Elliot laughed some more. He climbed slowly to his feet. He looked kind of dizzy to me. His eyes were darting from side to side.

Was it really a joke? Or did the flash of light knock him out somehow?

Weird.

"Cool invention," Elliot said. He picked up the light-stick and studied it. He raised it a few feet from his face and blew gently on it.

"No. It only works once," I told him. "It burns off the chemicals, so it won't light anymore."

He set it down on the table. "It's still totally cool. You make a lot of inventions like this?"

"Well, yeah," I said. "Mostly I just mix chemicals together to see what will happen."

He pushed back his hair and turned to the window. A beam of yellow sunlight poured onto the bedroom floor. "Jay, want to go outside?"

"Yeah," I said.

I led the way downstairs. "Just going out for a walk," I called to my parents. We stepped out the front door.

I felt a shiver of fear roll down my back. I searched the front yard for lawn gnomes. But I didn't see any.

Across the street, McClatchy stood on a tall ladder with hedge clippers in his hands. He was busy trimming the tall hedge and didn't see us as we walked past on the street.

I felt angry all over again. I pictured him kicking Mr. Phineas. I felt bad that I didn't get my revenge last night.

Elliot and I turned the corner and kept walking. The sunlight felt good on my face. The warm air smelled fresh. I started to calm down.

Elliot kicked a stone to the curb. "I kind of heard what you were talking about with your dad," he said.

I kept my eyes straight ahead. "Really?"

"Yeah. He sounded pretty steamed."

"He can get a little stressed sometimes," I said. "He's been on my case a lot lately."

Elliot stopped walking. We stood in the shade of a fat old tree. The tree limbs trembled above us in the wind, making the sunlight shimmer.

"Why has he been on your case?" Elliot asked. "Do you want to tell me about it?"

I swallowed. "Well . . ."

I didn't want to talk about it. I never talked about it with anyone.

Elliot's eyes locked on mine. He was waiting for my answer.

And suddenly, the words just blurted out of me: "I burned down our house."

22

Elliot's mouth dropped open. He started to talk but couldn't get the words out.

I led the way over to the wide tree trunk and sat down on the grass. The grass was still wet from the morning dew, but I didn't care. I decided to tell Elliot the whole story, the whole ugly story.

He sat down beside me, rested his back against the rough tree bark, and crossed his legs in front of him. "You're serious?" he said finally. "You really burned down your house?"

I nodded. "No joke."

"Jay, that's *horrible*. How did it happen?"

I took a deep breath. "My friend and I were in my room. Just messing around. I had a lab table in my old room, too. And lots of chemicals and stuff. I've been interested in chemistry since I was eight — four years now."

My chest felt fluttery. I could picture everything that happened so clearly.

"I had just started working on the light-stick. The thing I just showed you," I said. "I wanted to show it off to my friend. But I didn't have it quite right yet. I mean, I didn't have the chemicals right.

"But I held it up and blew on it really hard. And it exploded. I mean, it made a huge blast, like a bomb or something. A big flame shot out of it and . . . and . . ."

I had to stop to catch my breath. Even though we were in the shade, sweat poured down my face. My chest felt like a bird was fluttering its wings inside it.

"The flame shot out onto my lab table," I continued. "It . . . it set some chemicals on fire. The chemicals flamed up. With a roar, an incredible roar. The flames caught my bedroom curtains. And . . . and . . . my whole room was burning.

"My friend and I were coughing and choking on the black smoke. It was everywhere, all around us. We covered our faces with our shirt-sleeves, and we . . . we just ran out of the house.

"It . . . burned. The whole house. It just burned black. My friend and I . . . we were okay. We weren't burned or anything. But I was in shock. I mean, really in shock. I just couldn't believe that I'd done anything so horrible.

"But there was our house. Still smoking. The wood crackling. Just a big black pile. A big black pile . . ."

My voice trembled. I pictured our house. Everything we owned. Burned. Wrecked. Ashes.

"That's the story," I said finally. "That's what happened. I haven't told it to anyone — till now."

He stared at me. He didn't reply. He scratched the side of his face. I could see he was thinking hard.

"That's horrible," he said finally, in a soft whisper. "Just horrible. Jay, I . . . I don't know what to say. That's the worst thing I ever heard."

"Oh, wait," I said. "It gets worse. A lot worse."

I settled back against the tree trunk. I brushed a spider off the knee of my jeans. Down the street, a dog barked. I heard a lawnmower start up.

I felt strange. Kind of excited and very tense and wired. I guess because I'd never told this story to anyone.

I took another deep breath. "You see, my dad was president of the city council in our old town. It was, like, a really big deal. So, when I burned down our house, it was a *biiig* story. It was on TV and in the newspaper and people talked about it on the radio."

Elliot squinted at me. "Did they know it was an accident? It was an accident, right?"

I nodded. "The fire was a total accident. But I'd been in trouble before. You know. At school and stuff. Nothing serious. But a lot of people said I was mad at my dad and that's why I burned down the house."

Elliot shook his head. "Wow."

"So, my dad had to quit his job," I continued. "It was really bad around our house. I had to go to children's court. Talk about scary! We told the whole story to the judge six times. But she didn't believe me when I said it was an accident."

"Wow," Elliot repeated. "Wow."

"The judge said I was dangerous. She wanted to send me to some kind of youth prison." I stopped for a moment. This part of the story was hard to tell.

"But you changed her mind?" Elliot asked. "What did you do?"

"My dad made a deal with her," I replied. "The judge said if my family moved out of town . . . if we moved far away, she would drop all charges and let me go."

I sighed. "So . . . we moved, and here we are."

Elliot blinked a few times. I could see he was thinking hard again. "I have one question," he said finally. "You accidentally burned down your house because of one of those light-sticks you invented, right?"

"Right," I said.

"But you just showed me a light-stick. Why do your parents let you work on light-sticks after what happened?"

I put a finger to my lips. "*Shhhh*. They don't know about it. I had to sneak my chemistry set into our new house. They don't know I've gone back to working on light-sticks. It's a total secret."

"Whoa." Elliot shook his head. "Isn't that looking for trouble?"

"Not if I'm careful," I said. But then I added: "I try to be good. You know, I promised I'd be different here in our new home. And I'm really trying. But it's hard. Like my bike going into the quagmire, and that car accident yesterday. Sometimes accidents happen."

Elliot nodded. "I guess."

I climbed to my feet and brushed off the back of my jeans. "Hey, I promised my dad I'd walk the dog and then mow the back lawn," I said. "I'd better get going. But do you want to hang out after dinner? You know. Go to a movie or something?"

"Huh?" Elliot's mouth dropped open. He narrowed his eyes at me. "Did you forget, Jay? We can't go out at night. We can *never* go out at night."

Why not? Why is everyone afraid to go out at night?

Those are the questions I wanted to ask Elliot. But he hurried away, and I didn't get a chance.

Of course, he probably wouldn't answer anyway. He'd probably mutter, "You know." The way he always did.

Well . . . the whole thing was weird. There were definitely secrets here in my new town, secrets I didn't know the answers to.

But I'm going to find out, I told myself. *I'm going to find out what goes on here at night.*

I turned away from the fat tree trunk where Elliot and I had been sitting. I was still feeling a little tense. But I was glad I told Elliot the story of what had happened back home. It felt good to tell it to someone who would understand.

I took two steps — and then stopped.

A lawn gnome stood a few feet away. It had its back turned. I stared at its red coat pulled down over smooth white pants. Its painted black boots. The tall red hat tilted on its head.

That lawn gnome wasn't here before.

I know I didn't see it.

My whole body tensed. My hands balled into fists.

It's alive. It turned its back so I wouldn't know it was listening. But it was here listening to my whole story.

My fear gave way to anger. I could feel it start to burn in my chest.

I pictured the lawn gnomes last night. Scampering in the dark. Alive. Alive and vicious. They tried to hurt me. They tried to scare me.

I wanted to show them they couldn't mess with me.

I stared hard at the lawn gnome's back, feeling my anger rise.

And then I burst forward. Without making a sound, I made a leap at the gnome. I flew at it from behind — and tackled it hard around the waist.

"OWWWW." I let out a cry of pain as my shoulder slammed into the back of the lawn gnome.

My hands grabbed solid stone. Pain shot down my shoulder as I hit the hard body. The gnome didn't budge.

I slid to the ground. I lay in the grass, waiting for the waves of pain to fade.

Finally, I pulled myself to my feet and walked around to the front of the gnome. Its painted eyes stared blankly straight ahead. Its mouth was frozen open in a sick, red-lipped grin.

I tapped its hat. I pinched its stubby, round nose. I poked it in the eyes with two fingers.

Stone. Hard stone.

Not alive.

I must have looked like a nut job attacking a little statue!

I bent down and gazed into its eyes. Paint. Just paint. No one in there. No way it could possibly move. No way it could be alive.

But I knew they could come to life. I'd just spent the scariest night of my life watching them come to life and come after me.

How did it happen? Why?

The lawn gnomes were a mystery about this town I had to solve. Once again, I pictured Elliot's frightened face as he said, *We can't go out at night. We can never go out at night.*

Another mystery. I planned to solve it — tonight.

Of course, that night Kayla tried to talk me out of it. She paced back and forth in front of me in my room, swinging her red hair and shaking her head. "Jay, are you out of your mind?" she demanded.

"Maybe," I said. I sat on the edge of my bed and watched her storm around.

"If you go outside, you'll get in trouble — right?"

"Maybe," I said.

She stopped walking and stood over me with her arms crossed. "Is it worth it?"

"Maybe," I said.

"But you told Mom and Dad —"

"Kayla, there are too many weird things going on," I said. "Something isn't right about our new neighborhood."

She poked me in the chest. "Yes, something isn't right. It's *you*."

"Ha-ha." I rolled my eyes. I jumped to my feet and pushed past her, heading toward the bedroom door. "I'm not going outside to cause trouble. I'm not going to do anything bad at McClatchy's house. I promise."

"What *are* you going to do?"

"Just look around," I told her. "See if I can figure out what's up with all the lawn gnomes. See if I can learn why everyone is so terrified of going out at night."

She shook her head. "You know you shouldn't do this."

I grabbed two light-sticks and shoved them in my pocket. Then I hurried out of the room and down the stairs so I wouldn't hear any more of her warnings.

My sister is a big coward. She follows every rule. I guess some people like to follow rules. I'm not one of them.

I pulled open the front door and stepped outside.

Was I looking for trouble?

Maybe.

26

I saw a tiny slice of a moon in the sky, but it kept disappearing behind wisps of cloud. There was no breeze at all. The air was still. The trees in the front yard didn't move.

I stepped onto the porch and peered both ways. I expected to find lawn gnomes somewhere beside me.

But no. The porch swing stood in pale light from the streetlamp. The canvas chairs beside it were empty. No gnomes in sight.

I jumped down onto the grass. My parents' bedroom light still glowed. They were awake. I could see their shadows on the window shade.

I had to be quiet. I tiptoed down the middle of the yard. Dad's car was parked in the driveway. In the darkness, it reminded me of a large animal about to pounce.

Okay, yes, I was a little freaked. I mean, I don't have nerves of steel. I'm not a total coward like Kayla. But being out here late at night when

I knew it was against the rules . . . Well, it made my imagination go a little wild.

I turned away from it and gazed toward the street. There were no lawn gnomes in my front yard. I didn't see any at the curb.

I felt a chill at the back of my neck. The air was so still. As if everything had frozen in place.

I was the only thing moving. The only person out here. No cars moving on the street. No animal sounds or doors slamming or garage doors rumbling or footsteps or voices or birds chirping or crickets . . . or . . . *anything*!

Freaky, right?

I reached the curb and gazed into McClatchy's front yard. His house was pitch-black. Not a light on anywhere.

In the deep silence, my footsteps sounded deafening as I crossed the street and stepped onto McClatchy's driveway. I turned and peered down the long, tall hedge. McClatchy's two lawn gnomes usually stood together at the back of the hedge.

But, no. The hedge rose up like a black wall. I squinted hard. And saw only darkness.

I took a few cautious steps up McClatchy's driveway. Again, I felt a chill at the back of my neck. My throat tightened and my legs felt wobbly as I made my way toward the house.

Silence.

The only sound was my rapid breathing. My

eyes darted all around. I felt like a frightened rabbit. Every sense was alert.

Where have all the lawn gnomes gone?

It isn't really that late. Why isn't anyone else outside?

I squinted hard at McClatchy's front porch. I saw a stack of firewood logs piled at one end. A large axe leaned against the porch wall. A pair of tall black boots stood beside the door.

Suddenly, I froze. My breath caught in my chest.

A sound. I heard a sound.

The crunch of leaves. The soft *thud* of a footstep. Then another.

Every muscle in my body tightened. I forced myself to turn toward the sound.

I still couldn't see them in the darkness. But I could hear them.

The lawn gnomes. They were coming for me.

27

The tiny moon slid out from behind the clouds. Pale light washed over the lawn. The scrape of rapid footsteps grew louder.

I held my breath. And stared at a family of raccoons making their way across the grass. They kept their heads low. Their dark-ringed eyes stared straight ahead. There were five or six of them, walking rapidly in a straight line.

I couldn't help it. A laugh burst from my throat.

I'd been so frightened, I was shaking. And all because of a family of raccoons.

The lawn gnomes had vanished. Disappeared. Where had they gone? I didn't care. It was perfectly safe out here.

What were people afraid of? Raccoons?

An idea popped into my head. I decided to go to Elliot's house.

I'll drag Elliot outside with me. I'll show him there's nothing to be afraid of.

I trotted down to the street and turned away from McClatchy's yard. I remembered the houses looked a lot alike on Elliot's block. But I was pretty sure I remembered his. Third house from the corner.

I jogged along the side of the street. I gazed into every yard I passed. No lawn gnomes anywhere. I had seen at least two or three in front of every house. But now they had all vanished.

Weird. But so what?

It took me only a few minutes to reach Elliot's block. I heard a cat crying through an open window. Another house had the TV turned up really loud.

It was a block of small, square houses. I peered down the street. No one outside. Nothing moving.

I trotted up to the third house from the corner. I saw Elliot's bike leaning against one wall. And I saw Elliot through the front window. He was sitting at a table with a laptop glowing in front of him. I could see on the screen that he was playing a game.

I stepped up to the house and tapped on the window. He didn't hear me. He didn't turn around.

I tapped harder on the glass. Then I shouted: "Hey, Elliot — it's me."

He finally turned around. His eyes bulged with surprise. He came up close to the window and peered out at me for a long time.

Like he was seeing a ghost or something.

I waved for him to come to the front door. And I could see the fear in his eyes.

A few seconds later, he pulled the front door open just a crack. "Jay — what are you doing out there?"

"Having fun," I said. "Come on out."

He peeked out at me through the crack. I could only see one eye.

"Go home," he whispered. "Are you crazy? You shouldn't be out there."

"Come on, Elliot," I said. "I swear there's nothing to be afraid of."

"It's not allowed," he insisted. "Everyone knows it's not allowed."

"Everyone is wrong," I said. I pushed the front door open wider and grabbed his arm. "Come on out. It's an awesome night. Come on. Try it."

"I . . . don't think so," he said. He pulled back. "Maybe some other time. But I have to ask my parents. They —"

I wrapped my fingers around his wrist and tugged him out onto the front walk. His eyes bulged again, and he gazed all around.

"See? Perfectly safe," I said.

"Th-this is a big mistake," he stammered.

"No way," I said. "Let's take a walk. It's so totally cool. We're the only ones out here. It's like it's our own private world."

He swallowed hard. "I . . . don't . . . like this," he said. His eyes darted from side to side.

I pulled him to the street.

"What's that sound?" he cried.

"It's a cat," I told him. "Inside the house on the corner." I started to walk, waving for him to follow me. "Come on, dude. A short walk. Calm down. Really. We're the only ones out here. See?"

He held back. "But, Jay — you know the rules. You know what —"

I kept walking. I knew he'd follow me.

"Hey, wait up," he called. He came scrambling after me.

"Isn't this awesome?" I said. We crossed the street and turned onto the next block. "Isn't this totally awesome? Our own world?"

He poked me in the ribs.

"Hey." I spun around. "Why'd you do that?"

His chin trembled. His eyes were wide again. He pointed. "Uh . . . Jay . . . I don't think we're alone."

28

Gazing into the dark, I heard the thunder of footsteps.

The lawn gnomes seemed to appear from all directions. How many were there? Fifty? A hundred? An *army* of lawn gnomes!

They moved quickly. Their little boots pounded the pavement. Their tall caps bobbed and tilted under the pale moonlight. Their faces were shadowy and grim, eyes narrowed on Elliot and me.

We had no time to move. They surrounded us, forming a tight circle. I gazed from one unfriendly bearded face to the next.

They were a foot shorter than Elliot and me. But there was no way we could fight them. They closed in tightly, bumping their hard chests against us. Pushing us. Pushing until we were squeezed together.

They still hadn't spoken or made a sound. They crushed around us, squeezing us in the middle of their tight circle.

"Malfunction," one of them said finally, in a squeaky cartoon voice. "Malfunction."

He was staring at me as he said it.

"What do you *want*?" I shouted. "Go away! We haven't done anything to you!"

Elliot put a hand on my shoulder. "Careful," he whispered. "Don't get them angry."

"Angry?" I cried. "*I'm* the one who's angry."

"*Shhhhh*," Elliot warned. "I told you we're not allowed out here."

"Go away!" I screamed at them. "Leave us alone!"

I placed my hands on the shoulders of the gnome in front of me and tried to push him out of my way.

I guess that was a mistake. Because the gnomes all uttered angry cries at once. It sounded like dogs giving a warning bark.

And then the little guy shoved my hands off. He grabbed me by the waist — squeezed me hard in an iron grip — and *hoisted* me off the ground.

"Whoooa!" I let out a startled cry. The gnome was incredibly strong.

I tried to squirm and spin out of his hands. That only made him squeeze my waist tighter. I tried to hit him. My hands grabbed nothing but air. I couldn't escape.

Other gnomes reached for me. They held me high above their heads. And then I saw Elliot lifted off his feet.

He didn't put up too much of a struggle. I guess he was too frightened.

A few seconds later, the gnomes began to move. Elliot and I were helpless. Bumping along, held high over their pointed hats. I twisted and screamed and squirmed and thrashed my arms.

The army of gnomes bunched together like a herd of cattle. Moving in a straight line down the street with Elliot and me on our backs, prisoners.

"Let us down!" I screamed. I was so frightened, my voice came out in a high squeak.

They moved quickly, their boots thudding the pavement as they carried us along the dark, empty street. Their stone-hard fingers dug into my sides, into my back.

"Let us go!" I wailed. "Where are you taking us? What are you going to *do*?"

"Stop! Let us go!" I shouted. But they ignored my cries. The clatter of their boots on the pavement drowned out my terrified screams.

Elliot and I bumped along together. It was like being carried by a powerful ocean wave. And I saw no one else on the street, no one who could stop them or try to help us.

I could scream till my throat exploded and no one would hear.

The gnomes turned a corner. Tall trees passed overhead. I glanced over to Elliot. "Where are they taking us? Do you have any idea?"

His face was twisted in fear. "Jay, I know exactly where they are taking us," he said in a trembling voice. "They are taking us to the quagmire. They are going to throw us in."

"Huh?" A cry escaped my throat.

"That's the punishment for being out at night," Elliot said. "I . . . I tried to tell you."

"The punishment?" I cried. "For being outside? I don't understand. That makes no sense to me."

101

"Don't you remember *anything*?" Elliot demanded.

"Remember?"

"Yes. Jay, why are you acting so stupid? Everyone knows the lawn gnomes come alive at night. It's only *our* world during the day. But when it gets dark out, the gnomes take over. It's their world and — and — you should stop pretending you don't know all this."

I didn't get a chance to reply.

The gnomes stopped suddenly. I bounced hard in their hands. They lowered me slowly to the ground and placed me gently on my feet.

I gazed around. The moon floated high in the sky, sending down pale silvery light.

The quagmire gleamed in front of us. A shimmering, deadly lake. A lake of thick quicksand where it took only seconds to sink out of sight.

I shuddered.

I remembered my first time here. And I pictured Elliot and me sinking . . . sinking . . . And I thought of my lost bike, somewhere deep below the cold, smelly surface.

I took a deep breath. And made one last try at escape. I shot my arms out. Bent my knees. Tried to kick myself free.

But the gnomes held tight. I couldn't budge.

I turned and saw that Elliot was still held in the air. Four gnomes raised him high over their heads.

His eyes were wild with fright. "Help me!" he cried. "They're going to toss me in."

The gnomes moved forward, toward the lake of quicksand.

"Wait —" I uttered.

Gnomes pushed hard all around me so I couldn't move.

I watched in horror as the other gnomes carried Elliot to the edge of the quagmire. They raised him higher, ready to heave him in.

"Jay — help me! Help me! Please!" he wailed.

I had to do something. This was all my fault. *My fault.*

I had to do *something* to save my friend. But — what?

Suddenly, I had an idea.

30

"Help me!" Elliot screamed.

The gnomes rushed to the edge of the quag-mire, holding him high. They pulled back their arms, ready to heave him in feetfirst.

I twisted myself around. Gave myself a little room. Reached into my jeans pocket. And pulled out a light-stick.

Before a gnome could grab it away, I raised it to my face — and blew on it as hard as I could.

WHOOOOOSH.

The light-stick exploded in a blinding flash of fiery light. The sky lit up bright as day.

I held the light-stick high in front of me. And in its glowing light, I saw that my idea had worked.

The gnomes stood stiffly, frozen. Hard and still — like lawn gnomes. Lifeless once again.

"Yesss!" I raised my hands in a victory cry.

My thinking was correct: The gnomes came to life at night. But they froze in daylight.

And so, they froze in the bright light of my light-stick.

"Yesss!" I did a little victory dance. My invention saved our lives.

How long would the light-stick glow? How long could I keep the gnomes frozen?

I didn't know. We had to act fast before it got dark again. I slid past two gnomes to get to Elliot.

"Elliot? Hey — Elliot?"

I expected to see him run toward me. But to my shock, he was sprawled flat on his back on the ground.

When the light-stick flashed, did the gnomes drop him on his head?

I suddenly remembered what happened back in my bedroom. When I showed Elliot the light-stick for the first time, he fell to the floor when I flashed it.

He said he was only joking. But did bright light make Elliot faint?

Something weird was going on here.

I dropped beside him on the grass at the edge of the quagmire. "Elliot — wake up. Elliot. Come on. We have to run."

He didn't budge.

"Elliot — come on, dude."

The light dimmed. I heard some gnomes begin to groan and move.

"Elliot — please." I grabbed his arm and tugged. "Get up! Get UP! We don't have any time!"

And then I opened my mouth in a horrified scream.

His arm — it yanked off in my hands.

The whole arm ripped away from the shoulder. And . . . and . . .

Oh, noooo.

I saw wires and circuits and mechanical things. Inside Elliot's arm!

"Oh, wow," I murmured. I gaped at the loose arm, at the wires and cables inside it.

"Elliot — what *is* this? What ARE you? I — I don't understand!"

He slowly raised his head. He turned to me. His eyes slid back and forth. "Malfunction," he said.

"Huh? Elliot? Please —" I begged.

"Malfunction," he repeated. "Malfunction. Malfunction . . ."

"What's *wrong* with you?" I cried. "Get up! Stop saying that! We have to get away from here!"

The quagmire bubbled suddenly. It made a sound like a loud burp.

"Elliot —"

"Malfunction. Malfunction." His eyes darted faster from side to side.

The light-stick was dead now. Darkness returned. I heard a rustling behind me.

I turned and saw the lawn gnomes stretching

their arms above their heads. Yawning. Waking up.

I let go of Elliot's arm. It rolled over the grass. "Malfunction. Malfunction."

I jumped to my feet. My heart pounded so hard, I could barely breathe.

Elliot's voice rang in my ear, repeating that word over and over. I knew I couldn't save him.

But I had to try to save myself.

The gnomes all stood now. They moved quickly. Their eyes were all on me. Their shadowy faces were menacing, all scowls and clenched jaws beneath their beards.

I had one more light-stick in my pocket. I tugged it out.

I knew I had to put the gnomes back to sleep. It was my only chance to escape them.

I raised the light-stick close to my face. I sucked in a deep breath — and blew hard.

Nothing happened.

It didn't light.

31

I took a deep breath and blew on it again.

No. Not happening.

My hand trembled as I turned it over and blew on the other end of the stick.

No. It didn't light. Maybe it was one I'd already used in my room.

With a cry, I tossed the light-stick into the quagmire. It landed with a soft *thunk* and sank immediately.

Elliot lay lifelessly at my feet, his mechanical arm beside him. He had finally stopped repeating the word *malfunction*. His mouth hung open, and his eyes stared blankly up at the pale sliver of a moon above the trees.

Run, I told myself.

I gazed around, frantically searching for the best escape path. But the gnomes had me surrounded. Once again, they'd formed a circle. They were closing in.

And then I saw someone . . . Someone standing at the edge of the quagmire, watching me.

Not a gnome. Not a gnome.

It took me a few seconds to recognize who it was.

And then I opened my mouth and uttered a cry:

"HELP me! Please — HELP me!"

32

She didn't move. She had her hands pushed deep into the pockets of her jacket. Her hair fluttered in the breeze.

"Kayla — go get help!" I pleaded, my voice high with panic and surprise.

She took a few steps toward me. Her eyes glowed in the moonlight. Finally, she spoke. "I followed you here."

"Good! You — you've got to help me," I stammered. "The gnomes . . . They carried Elliot and me here. They want to throw us in the quagmire."

Kayla's face was hidden in shadow. She spoke in a calm, low voice, nearly a whisper: "You broke the rules, Jay. We're not supposed to go out at night."

"I . . . I didn't know," I said. "I didn't realize. Kayla — get help! Hurry!"

"The lawn gnomes come alive at night," Kayla said. "It's their world at night. Everyone knows that, Jay."

"But . . . Elliot," I stammered. "I thought he was my friend. But he's some kind of robot or something."

Kayla stared straight ahead. "So?"

"So?" I cried. "What do you mean? It's *horrible*! Aren't you even surprised?"

She shook her head.

I glanced away. The lawn gnomes were moving again. Tightening their circle. Growling and grumbling and uttering low threats.

I had only seconds to act.

"Kayla, I don't know what to do!" I cried. "Aren't you frightened, too?"

She shook her head again.

"Can you help me?" I wailed. "Can you think of something? Can you help?"

"I'm so sorry, Jay," she said. She moved closer and I saw the sad expression on her face. "I'm so sorry. I can't help you."

"Why?" I cried in a total panic. "Why can't you help me?"

Her eyes locked on mine. "Because I'm imaginary," she said. "I'm your imaginary sister. So how can I help you?"

33

Everything started to spin. As if I was on some kind of crazed, out-of-control carousel.

I shut my eyes but it didn't stop my dizziness.

Kayla is imaginary?

Why did she say that? It can't be true — can it?

Am I totally crazy?

I opened my eyes. "Kayla, I don't understand. I —"

She was gone. Vanished.

I staggered forward and nearly tripped over Elliot.

My friend was a robot and my sister was imaginary. This was too much to deal with. My head felt about to explode.

I knew I should run. But I couldn't force my legs to move.

I stood frozen there, my head spinning, as the gnomes swarmed around me. They grumbled and groaned in low voices and shoved me into the center of their circle.

Caught in the middle of the crowd, I was pushed one way, then the other.

"Malfunction," a gnome said in a harsh whisper. "Malfunction. Malfunction."

And they all picked up the chant.

I let out a cry and covered my ears. I tried to shout over their tinny, hoarse voices so I wouldn't have to hear that word anymore.

And without thinking about it another second, I lowered my shoulder like a football running back. And I jammed it into the gnome closest to me.

He uttered a *yip* and toppled to one side. As he stumbled, he knocked over the gnome next to him, who fell and sent another gnome sprawling to the grass.

A whole bunch of gnomes went down like bowling pins. And I took off, running with my shoulder down.

I butted another gnome hard. He let out a startled groan as he flew off his feet and sailed into two or three other lawn gnomes.

Yessss!

Gnomes grabbed at me. Flew at me. Tried to tackle me.

I dodged and ducked and slid from their grasp. My sneakers slapped the grass hard as I ran . . . away from the shouting gnomes . . . away from the disgusting quagmire.

A gnome dove to tackle me. I swerved away from him, and he sailed onto the ground on his belly.

Two more lawn gnomes came at me. I reached out and swiped their long red hats. I tossed the hats on the grass and kept running. They forgot about me and dove to retrieve their hats.

I was panting hard now, but I didn't slow down. I ran through the darkness, tall black trees all around. No one in sight. No one.

Up ahead, I could see a block of small houses. My heart pounding, I glanced back. No gnomes. No gnomes behind me.

I had outrun them. I had won.

I wanted to jump for joy. I wanted to scream and shout out my victory.

But I kept running. And listening for their raspy voices, their tapping footsteps.

I recognized the houses on the block. I knew I was three or four blocks from home.

Keep going, Jay. Don't slow down.

I turned the corner. My breath came out in rapid wheezes. I recognized Elliot's house as I ran past it. I wondered if his parents were worried about him.

But that only brought questions to my mind: If Elliot was a robot, did he *have* parents? Why did he pretend to be human? Was he only pretending to be my friend?

I couldn't stop to think about it. I had to keep running.

I was only a block from my house now. One block from safety.

I slid on some leaves. Caught my balance. And stopped with a gasp as I saw *more* lawn gnomes. Dozens of them. Moving toward me, swarming from all directions.

I lowered my shoulder to bump them out of my way. Maybe I could run right through them. Escape as I had before.

But no. I didn't have the strength. I'd used up all my energy. I had nothing left. Nothing.

I stood there panting, my whole body aching. I couldn't put up a fight.

Buzzing like excited bees, the lawn gnomes circled me. The circle tightened. Once again, I was raised off the ground. Lifted high by several gnomes.

I lay captured, helpless, staring up at the sliver of moon. It looked like a grin. It looked like the moon was laughing at me as this new bunch of gnomes gleefully carried me down the street.

Back to the quagmire.

They held me tightly above their heads and carried me back to the disgusting quicksand pit. And as I frantically tried to gather my strength, I saw that there were *hundreds* of them now.

Hundreds of gnomes, cheering and shouting and buzzing and pumping their little fists in the air.

"No! Please. Please!" I begged as they hoisted me toward the deadly lake.

But no one could hear my cries over the joyful shouts of the gnomes.

It was like a celebration. Why were they so happy to dump me in the quicksand? Just because I stepped outdoors at night?

"Please! Please!"

I twisted and squirmed. But their little hands dug into my skin and held me in place.

They carried me to the edge of the quagmire. They lifted me higher.

I heard gnomes cheering. And laughing.

And then they heaved me hard. I felt myself fly from their hands. I sailed headfirst through the air. Screaming, I landed with a *splaaat*.

I choked as the cold, lumpy glop poured into my open mouth.

I struggled to swim. I slapped my arms on the surface of the wet gunk. But I couldn't keep myself up.

Choking, I sank fast ... down ... down into the cold, wet darkness.

34

Darkness all around. A deep black I'd never seen before.

I couldn't breathe. The thick sand clogged my throat.

I felt myself sinking. Rapidly sinking deeper into the quagmire.

This isn't fair, I told myself. *I didn't know the rule. I didn't know the penalty for being out after dark.*

How can this be happening to me?

I tried to thrash my arms. Tried frantically to pull myself to the surface of the cold quicksand.

But I didn't have the strength. I gave up. I let my arms float at my sides as I sank deeper . . . deeper.

Suddenly, I saw a flash of light. The darkness gave way to a blinding white light.

My brain is exploding.

I felt something grab me from underneath. Something wrapped around my stomach, my chest, my legs.

It gripped me tightly. And held on.

The biting fish! The fish with legs.

I remembered how they chomped at my legs, bit big holes in my jeans. How they leaped from the sand, snapping their pointed teeth.

Was I going to end up as *fish food*?

No. Gripped in horror, I realized I was rising through the muck. The thing that wrapped around me — was it some kind of net? It pulled me higher.

The wet sand washed over me as I rose. It seemed to take forever. But soon I popped above the surface.

I felt the cool, fresh air on my face. I coughed, and sucked in a deep breath. And then another.

My eyes were still closed. They were covered in gunk. I raised my hands and wiped frantically at my face.

Finally, I opened my eyes. I saw the pack of lawn gnomes at the edge of the quagmire. They worked a long pole that stretched toward me. The pole held the net that was wrapped around me.

They swung it hard, and I went sailing over the quicksand. I landed on my back on the grass.

First the gnomes tossed me into the quagmire. Then they used the big net to rescue me.

Why?

Still gasping for breath, I pulled myself to my feet. I stumbled and fell back to my knees. I was completely tangled in the net.

Two gnomes came forward and started to pull the net off me. My clothes felt sticky and damp. Wet sand clung to my skin.

Finally, the net fell away. The two gnomes stepped back.

The lawn gnomes stood silently in a group. They stared at me. They had weird expressions on their bearded faces, as if they expected me to speak.

But I didn't know what they wanted me to say. I think I was still in shock. Still shaken by sinking so deep in the quicksand. Thinking that I was going to die down there.

As I stared back at the group of gnomes, I heard footsteps. The gnomes stepped aside.

And I saw Mom and Dad making their way through the crowd.

My mouth dropped open. I cried out, my voice hoarse from the sand I'd swallowed:

"Mom? Dad? What are you doing here?"

And then I saw Elliot and McClatchy walking behind them.

Their faces were all grim. They didn't speak.

I uttered a startled cry. "What is *happening*?"

Mom and Dad and McClatchy stopped in front of
the gnomes. Elliot walked closer, to the edge
of the quagmire.

"Huh? Are . . . are you okay?" I stammered.

He nodded. A grin spread over his face.

"But your arm —" I cried.

He held out his arm. He swung it up and
down. He squeezed the fingers into a fist. "No
problem," he said. "I'm all fixed. Everything
works fine."

Mom and Dad stepped up beside him. Their
faces were tight with worry.

"Are you okay?" Mom asked, her eyes studying me.

"We've been very worried about you," Dad
said.

I blinked. I still had grains of sand in my eye-
lashes. "Worried about me?" I said. "Why?"

"We couldn't get your programming to work,"
Dad answered.

I gasped. "My *what*?"

"Your programming," Dad repeated. "You were off track. We all tried to reset you. But you were completely malfunctioning."

Malfunctioning?

"But — but — but —" I couldn't speak. I just sputtered.

"The gnomes had the idea to scare you," Dad said.

"That's right," Mom added. "Sometimes a good scare will shake you back online."

The gnomes all began to mutter and nod their heads.

"But that's *crazy*!" I cried. "I —"

"We had to do something," Mom insisted. "We were desperate. We didn't want to lose you."

I stared at McClatchy standing behind my parents with his hands in his pockets. Why was he here? Was he part of this whole plan to scare me?

"I don't get it," I told them. "I didn't need a scare. I'm perfectly okay."

The gnomes began to mutter again.

"I hope you're right," Mom said, clasping her hands in front of her. "I really do."

Dad walked up and put his hand on my shoulder. "Let's give you a simple test," he said.

I gazed up at him. "A test?"

He nodded. "Answer this question: What is your name?"

I laughed. "Huh? My name? You're joking, right? Why are you asking such a totally easy question?"

Dad squeezed my shoulder. "Go ahead. Just answer it. What is your name?"

I made a face at him. "My name is Pul-Mar, of course."

Mom and Dad both let out loud sighs. Elliot clapped his hands. McClatchy cheered and pumped a fist in the air.

"Oh, thank goodness!" Mom cried. "We don't have to call you Jay anymore. Pul-Mar. That's your name. And where do we live?"

"Another easy one," I muttered. "We live on Polovia. Planet of the Lawn Gnomes."

36

Everyone cheered again. The lawn gnomes jumped up and down and tossed their red caps in the air. McClatchy pumped his fist.

Mom and Dad rushed forward and hugged me tight. Mom had tears in her eyes. "We were so worried about you, Pul-Mar," she said in a trembling voice.

Dad agreed. "All of a sudden, you started telling people your name was Jay. And you said you came from some strange planet we never heard of. It was called Earth."

I laughed. "Jay? What a stupid name!"

"And where did you come up with that weird planet?" McClatchy asked.

"Earth?" I thought hard. "I think I read about a planet called Earth in a sci-fi story. It doesn't really exist."

"Of *course* it doesn't," Dad said. "But you told everyone you lived there."

"Weird," I murmured. "Totally weird."

"You started acting very strange," Mom said. "You began playing jokes on people and pulling dumb pranks."

"That definitely isn't in your programming," Dad said.

"And you made up an imaginary sister for yourself," Mom added. "You called her Kayla."

I blinked. "Really? I did? That's crazy. I never had a sister-noid."

Elliot stepped forward. "You told me you were new here," he said. "But that's not true. You've lived in this neighborhood your whole life."

I nodded. "Yeah, I know."

"And you said you burned your house down," Elliot continued. "But I knew that couldn't be true. I knew you loved mixing chemicals. And I knew you made light-sticks. But the houses on Polovia are all built of stumis. And stumis can't burn."

"Of course stumis can't burn," I said.

And suddenly, it all came back to me. The truth about life on Polovia and who I was. Everything. It just flashed back into my mind.

Me, my parents, Elliot, McClatchy — we're all mecha-noids. We were built by the lawn gnomes to work for them during the day, before they come to life every night.

"I get it," I said. "I remember everything now."

The gnomes cheered again and tossed their caps. I guess they were happy their scare cure worked.

I waved to them and shouted thanks. Then I followed my parents home.

My gears creaked and my circuits groaned. I was exhausted. What a long night!

I said good night to my parents and hurried upstairs to my room. I clicked on the light. To my surprise, someone was waiting for me there.

"Mr. Phineas!" I cried.

I started across the room to him. But I stopped short when he began to *speak*.

"We have to get out of here, Jay," the dog rasped in a throaty, deep voice. "We have to find a way back to Earth."

I gasped. "Huh? Earth?" I squinted at the dog. "You — you speak?"

Mr. Phineas nodded. "No time to explain. We have to get moving. We have to go back home."

"To Earth?" I cried. "That's an imaginary planet. I can't do that! That's totally crazy."

The dog tilted his head and stared at me. "Come on, Jay — who are you going to believe? Them? Or your dog?"

The list continues with book #2

SON OF SLAPPY

Here's a sneak peek!

My name is Jackson Stander. I'm twelve, and I know a secret.

You don't have to ask. I'm going to share my secret with you. When I tell you what it is, you might laugh at me.

My sister Rachel laughs at me. She rolls her eyes and groans and calls me a goodie-goodie.

But I don't care. Rachel is in trouble all the time, and I'm not. And that's because of my secret, which I'm going to share with you now:

It's a lot easier to be good than to be bad.

That's the whole thing. You're probably shaking your head and saying, "What's the big deal? What kind of crazy secret is that?"

It's simple. Let me explain. I try hard to do the right thing all the time. I try to be nice to everyone, and work hard in school, and be cheerful and kind, and help people when I can, and just be a good dude.

This makes Rachel sick. She's always poking her finger down her throat and making gagging sounds whenever I say or do something nice.

Rachel is a real sarcastic kid and a trouble-maker. She likes to argue with her teacher, and she gets into fights with kids in her class. She hates it when the teachers say, "Why can't you be more like your brother, Jackson?"

What does she call me? She calls me *Robot*. She says I'm some kind of goodie-goodie machine.

You've probably guessed that Rachel and I don't get along that well, even though she's just a year younger than me.

We both look a lot alike, too. We're kind of average height. We have straight brown hair and brown eyes, and we both have freckles on our noses and dimples when we smile.

Rachel hates her dimples and her freckles. She says she hates it that she looks more like Dad than like Mom. Of course, that doesn't make Dad very happy. He calls Rachel *Problem Child*. Mom scolds him every time he says it.

But she *is* a problem child. Mainly, she's *my* problem because she's always in my face. And she's always testing me, teasing me. Trying to make me lose it, blow up, get steamed, start to shout or fight.

Rachel's mission in life is to get me in trouble with Mom and Dad. She's always trying to make me look bad. But she's so lame. There's *no way* she can win.

A few weeks ago, she was doing an art project in her room and spilled red paint on her floor. She went running to Mom and said, "Jackson was messing around with my paint, and look what he did."

Of course, Mom didn't believe her for a second. Why would I be messing around with her paint?

Last night before dinner, Rachel was helping Mom carry the food to the table. She tripped over Sparky, our cat, dropped a platter of chicken — and it went flying all over the floor.

"Jackson tripped me!" Rachel told Mom.

I was standing all the way across the room. How lame was that?

But Rachel keeps trying.

Now, please don't get me wrong. I'm not perfect. If I told you I'm perfect, that would be obnoxious. Besides, no one is perfect.

I just try to do my best. I really do believe it's easier to be good than bad.

It's something I knew from the time I was a tiny kid.

And then something happened.

Something happened, and I turned bad. I turned very bad. No. Let's tell the truth. I, Jackson Stander, became *evil*.

And that's what this story is all about.

We have two canaries at the YC. I gave them their names — Pete and Repete. I can't really tell which one is which, but I pretend.

After school on Wednesday, I was showing a bunch of kids how to pick the canaries up in your hand when you want to clean their cage.

YC stands for Youth Center. Actually, it's called the Morton Applegate, Jr. Borderville Youth Center. But no one remembers who Morton Applegate, Jr. is. And everyone knows we live in the town of Borderville. So people just call it the YC.

A lot of little kids go to the YC after school. They stay till their parents pick them up after work.

The YC playroom is very bright and cheerful. The walls are shiny red and yellow with funny cows and sheep painted upside down all over them, as if it was raining cows and sheep. The room has shelves to the ceiling, crammed with games and books and art supplies and puzzles and all kinds of great toys for the little kids.

There are stacks of car tires to bounce and climb on. A big flatscreen for playing video games. A fish tank, a rabbit cage, and the canary cage. Plenty of cool stuff to keep the kids busy till their parents arrive.

I like to go there after school when I don't have my piano lessons or tennis practice. I go to help out with the little kids. It's fun to play and read with them. The kids are funny, and they treat me like I'm a big deal.

There's a cute, chubby red-haired kid everyone calls Froggy because he's got a funny, scratchy voice. Froggy is my favorite. He's goofy and says the dumbest things to make everyone laugh. If I had a little brother, I'd like him to be Froggy.

Froggy and another favorite of mine — a tiny little blond-haired girl named Nikki — were watching as I reached into the canary cage. Nikki is very shy and quiet and speaks in a tiny little mouse voice. She has a sad face most of the time. But I know how to make her laugh.

"You have to move your hand in very slowly," I told them. "If you move too fast, you'll scare the canary, and it will start fluttering and flapping and cheeping like crazy."

Froggy, Nikki, and a few other kids watched silently as I tugged open the birdcage door. I slowly slid my open hand into the cage and moved it toward Pete.

"Sshhhh," I whispered. "You have to be very quiet and very careful." The canary stared at me from his wooden perch. The other one, head tilted to one side, watched from the swing.

"If you squeeze it too hard, will it explode?" Froggy asked in a raspy whisper. "I saw that in a cartoon."

"We don't want it to explode," I whispered. "We have to be very gentle."

I opened my hand and prepared to wrap it around the canary. The bird cheeped softly but didn't move. I held my breath and reached forward.

And someone right behind me screamed, "**BOO!**"

The canary squawked, fluttered out of my grasp — and darted out the open cage door.

My heart skipped a beat. I swung around. I saw my sister, Rachel, standing behind me, a grin on her face. Guess who shouted *Boo*?

The canary flew up to the ceiling.

Kids shouted in surprise. They chased after it.

The frightened canary flew in wild circles, round and round the room. It darted low. "Catch it!" I cried. "Somebody —"

Hands grabbed at the tiny yellow bird. It swooped high again. And then headed toward the far wall. Kids shrieked and ran after it.

"Nooo!" A scream burst from my throat. I could see where it was flying. "Close the window!" I shouted. "Hurry! Close the window!"

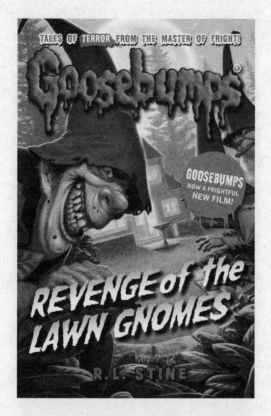

Turn the page for a peek at another
all-terrifying thrill ride from R.L. Stine.

Clack, Clack, Clack.

The ping-pong ball clattered over the basement floor. "Yes!" I cried as I watched Mindy chase after it.

It was a hot, sticky June afternoon. The first Monday of summer vacation. And Joe Burton had just made another excellent shot.

That's me. Joe Burton. I'm twelve. And there is nothing I love better than slamming the ball in my older sister's face and making her chase after it.

I'm not a bad sport. I just like to show Mindy that she's not as great as she thinks she is.

You might guess that Mindy and I do not always agree on things. The fact is, I'm really not like anyone else in my family.

Mindy, Mom, and Dad are all blond, skinny, and tall. I have brown hair. And I'm kind of pudgy and short. Mom says I haven't had my growth spurt yet.

So I'm a shrimp. And it's hard for me to see over the ping-pong net. But I can still beat Mindy with one hand tied behind my back.

As much as I love to win, Mindy hates to lose. And she doesn't play fair at all. Every time I make a great move, she says it doesn't count.

"Joe, *kicking* the ball over the net is not legal," she whined as she scooped out the ball from under the couch.

"Give me a break!" I cried. "All the ping-pong champions do it. They call it the Soccer Slam."

Mindy rolled her huge green eyes. "Oh, puhlease!" she muttered. "My serve."

Mindy is weird. She's probably the weirdest fourteen-year-old in town.

Why? I'll tell you why.

Take her room. Mindy arranges all her books in alphabetical order — by author. Do you believe it?

And she fills out a card for each one. She files them in the top drawer of her desk. Her own private card catalog.

If she could, she'd probably cut the tops off the books so they'd be all the same size.

She is *so* organized. Her closet is organized by color. All the reds come first. Then the oranges.

Then the yellows. Then come the greens, blues, and purples. She hangs her clothes in the same order as the rainbow.

And at dinner, she eats around her plate clockwise. Really! I've watched her. First her mashed potatoes. Then all her peas. And then her meat loaf. If she finds one pea in her mashed potatoes, she totally loses it!

Weird. Really weird.

Me? I'm not organized. I'm cool. I'm not serious like my sister. I can be pretty funny. My friends think I'm a riot. Everyone does. Except Mindy.

"Come on, serve already," I called out. "Before the end of the century."

Mindy stood on her side of the table, carefully lining up her shot. She stands in exactly the same place every time. With her feet exactly the same space apart. Her footprints are worn into the floor.

"Ten–eight and serving," Mindy finally called out. She always calls out the score before she serves. Then she swung her arm back.

I held the paddle up to my mouth like a microphone. "She pulls her arm back," I announced. "The crowd is hushed. It's a tense moment."

"Joe, stop acting like a jerk," she snapped. "I have to concentrate."

I love pretending I'm a sports announcer. It drives Mindy nuts.

Mindy pulled her arm back again. She tossed the Ping-Pong ball up into the air. And . . .

"A spider!" I screamed. "On your shoulder!"

"*Yaaaiiii!*" Mindy dropped the paddle and began slapping her shoulder furiously. The ball clattered onto the table.

"Gotcha!" I cried. "My point."

"No way!" Mindy shouted angrily. "You're just a cheater, Joe." She smoothed the shoulders of her pink T-shirt carefully. She picked up the ball and swatted it over the net.

"At least I'm a *funny* cheater!" I replied. I twirled around in a complete circle and belted the ball. It bounced once on my side before sailing over the net.

"Foul," Mindy announced. "You're always fouling."

I waved my paddle at her. "Get a life," I said. "It's a game. It's supposed to be fun."

"I'm beating you," Mindy replied. "That's fun."

I shrugged. "Who cares? Winning isn't everything."

"Where did you read that?" she asked. "In a bubble gum comic?" Then she rolled her eyes again. I think someday her eyes are going to roll right out of her head!

I rolled my eyes, too — back into my head until only the whites showed. "Neat trick, huh?"

"Cute, Joe," Mindy muttered. "Really cute. You'd better watch out. One day your eyes might not come back down. Which would be an improvement!"

"Lame joke," I replied. "Very lame."

Mindy lined up her feet carefully again.

"She's in her serve position," I spoke into my paddle. "She's nervous. She's . . ."

"Joe!" Mindy whined. "Quit it!"

She tossed the ping-pong ball into the air. She swung the paddle, and —

"Gross!" I shouted. "What's that big green glob hanging out of your nose?"

Mindy ignored me this time. She tapped the ball over the net.

I dove forward and whacked it with the tip of my paddle. It spun high over the net and landed in the corner of the basement. Between the washing machine and the dryer.

Mindy jogged after the ball on her long, thin legs. "Hey, where's Buster?" she called out. "Wasn't he sleeping next to the dryer?"

Buster is our dog. A giant black Rottweiler with a head the size of a basketball. He loves snoozing on the old sleeping bag we keep in the corner of the basement. Especially when we're down here playing Ping-Pong.

Everyone is afraid of Buster. For about three seconds. Then he starts licking them with his long, wet tongue. Or rolls onto his back and begs to have his belly scratched.

"Where is he, Joe?" Mindy bit her lip.

"He's around here somewhere," I replied. "Why are you always worrying about Buster? He weighs over a hundred pounds. He can take care of himself."

Mindy frowned. "Not if Mr. McCall catches him. Remember what he said the last time Buster chomped on his tomato plants?"

Mr. McCall is our next-door neighbor. Buster loves the McCalls' yard. He likes to nap under their huge, shady elm tree.

And dig little holes all over their lawn. And sometimes big holes.

And snack in their vegetable garden.

Last year, Buster dug up every head of Mr. McCall's lettuce. And ate his biggest zucchini plant for dessert.

I guess that's why Mr. McCall hates Buster. He said the next time he catches him in his garden, he's going to turn him into fertilizer.

My dad and Mr. McCall are the two best gardeners in town. They're nuts about gardening. Totally nuts.

I think working in a garden is kind of fun, too. But I don't let that get around. My friends think gardening is for nerds.

Dad and Mr. McCall are always battling it out at the annual garden show. Mr. McCall usually takes first place. But last year, Dad and I won the blue ribbon for our tomatoes.

That drove Mr. McCall crazy. When Dad's

name was announced, Mr. McCall's face turned as red as our tomatoes.

So Mr. McCall is desperate to win this year. He starting stocking up on plant food and bug spray months ago.

And he planted something that nobody else in North Bay grows. Strange orange-green melons called casabas.

Dad says that Mr. McCall has made a big mistake. He says the casabas will never grow any bigger than tennis balls. The growing season in Minnesota is too short.

"McCall's garden loses," I declared. "Our tomatoes are definitely going to win again this year. And thanks to my special soil, they'll grow as big as beach balls!"

"So will your head," Mindy shot back.

I stuck out my tongue and crossed my eyes. It seemed like a good reply.

"Whose serve is it?" I asked. Mindy was taking so long, I lost track.

"It's still my serve," she replied, carefully placing her feet.

We were interrupted by footsteps. Heavy, booming footsteps on the stairs behind Mindy.

"Who is that?" Mindy cried.

And then he appeared behind her. And my eyes nearly bulged right out of my head.

"Oh, no!" I screamed. "It's . . . McCall!"

"Joe!" he roared. The floor shook as he stomped toward Mindy.

All the color drained from Mindy's face. Her hand grasped her paddle so tightly that her knuckles turned white. She tried to swing around to look behind her, but she couldn't. Her feet were frozen in her ping-pong-ball footprints.

McCall's hands balled into two huge fists, and he looked really, really angry.

"I'm going to get you. And this time I'm going to win. Throw me a paddle."

"You jerk!" Mindy sputtered. "I — I knew it wasn't *Mr.* McCall. I knew it was Moose."

Moose is Mr. McCall's son and my best friend. His real name is Michael, but everyone calls him Moose. Even his parents.

Moose is the biggest kid in the whole sixth grade. And the strongest. His legs are as thick as tree trunks. And so is his neck. And he's very, very loud. Just like his dad.

Mindy can't stand Moose. She says he's a gross slob.

I think he's cool.

"Yo, Joe!" Moose bellowed. "Where's my paddle?" His big arm muscles bulged as he reached out to grab mine.

I pulled my hand back. But his beefy hand slapped my shoulder so hard that my head nearly rolled off.

"Whoaaa!" I yelped.

Moose let out a deep laugh that shook the basement walls. And then he ended it with a burp.

"Moose, you're disgusting," Mindy groaned.

Moose scratched his dark brown crew cut. "Gee, thanks, Mindy."

"Thanks for what?" she demanded.

"For this." He reached out and snatched the paddle right out of her hand.

Moose swung Mindy's paddle around wildly in the air. He missed a hanging lamp by an inch. "Ready for a real game, Joe?"

He threw the ping-pong ball into the air and drew his powerful arm back. *Wham!* The ball rocketed across the room. It bounced off two walls and flew back over the net toward me.

"Foul!" Mindy cried. "That's not allowed."

"Cool!" I exclaimed. I dove for the ball and missed. Moose has an amazing serve.

Moose slammed the ball again. It shot over the net and whacked me in the chest.

Thwock!

"Hey!" I cried. I rubbed the stinging spot.

"Good shot, huh?" He grinned.

"Yeah. But you're supposed to hit the table," I told him.

Moose pumped his fat fists into the air. "Super Moose!" he bellowed. "Strong as a superhero!"

My friend Moose is a pretty wild guy. Mindy says he's a total animal. I think he's just got a lot of enthusiasm.

I served while he was still throwing his arms around.

"Hey! No fair!" he declared. Moose charged the table and clobbered the ball. And flattened it into a tiny white pancake.

I groaned. "That's ball number fifteen for this month," I announced.

I grabbed the little pancake and tossed it into a blue plastic milk crate on the floor. The crate was piled high with dozens of flattened Ping-Pong balls.

"Hey! I think you broke your record!" I declared.

"All right!" Moose exclaimed. He leaped on top of the Ping-Pong table and began jumping up and down. "Super Moose!" he yelled.

"Stop it, you jerk!" Mindy screamed. "You're going to break the table." She covered her face with her hands.

"Super Moose! Super Moose!" he chanted.

The ping-pong table swayed. Then it sagged under his weight. He was even starting to get on my nerves now. "Moose, get off! Get off!" I wailed.

"Who's going to make me?" he demanded.

Then we all heard a loud, sharp *craaaaack*.

"You're breaking it!" Mindy shrieked. "Get off!"

Moose scrambled off the table. He lurched toward me, holding his hands straight out like the zombie monster we'd seen in *Killer Zombie from Planet Zero* on TV. "Now I'm going to destroy you!"

Then he hurled himself at me.

As he smashed into me, I staggered back and fell onto the dusty cement floor.

Moose jumped onto my stomach and pinned me down. "Say 'Moose's tomatoes are the best!'" he ordered. He bounced up and down on my chest.

"Moo-Moose's," I wheezed. "Tomat . . . I can't . . . breathe . . . really . . . help."

"Say it!" Moose insisted. He placed his powerful hands around my neck. And squeezed.

"*Ugggggh*," I gagged. I couldn't breathe. I couldn't move.

My head rolled to the side.

"Moose!" I heard Mindy shriek. "Let him go! Let him go! What have you done to him?"

About the Author

R.L. Stine's books are read all over the world. So far, his books have sold more than 300 million copies, making him one of the most popular children's authors in history. Besides Goosebumps, R.L. Stine has written the teen series Fear Street and the funny series Rotten School, as well as the Mostly Ghostly series, The Nightmare Room series, and the two-book thriller *Dangerous Girls*. R.L. Stine lives in New York with his wife, Jane, and Minnie, his King Charles spaniel. You can learn more about him at www.RLStine.com.

The Original Bone-Chilling Series

The Original Bone-Chilling Series